The enemy gunners surged toward the Executioner

Bolan was up and moving by the time his first two kills collapsed in front of him, backtracking toward the bungalow where he had hidden when he triggered the explosions. He circled behind it, moving like the shadow of a night prowler.

Go! Go! Go!

He keyed another blast, thirty yards behind him, and kept on running, seeking targets. It was all about momentum now, taking advantage of his lead, and anything that moved was Bolan's prey.

What was it Mae West had said? "So many men, so little time." But Mae had had her own technique, nothing in common with the Executioner's.

When Bolan screwed an enemy, that enemy stayed screwed, and there were no complaints.

The dead were good that way.

MACK BOLAN ®

The Executioner

DON PENDLETON'S
EXECUTIONER®
THE
CALL TO ARMS

THE ★ AMERICAN TRILOGY BOOK III

A GOLD EAGLE BOOK FROM
WORLDWIDE®

TORONTO • NEW YORK • LONDON
AMSTERDAM • PARIS • SYDNEY • HAMBURG
STOCKHOLM • ATHENS • TOKYO • MILAN
MADRID • WARSAW • BUDAPEST • AUCKLAND

First edition August 1997
ISBN 0-373-64224-5

Special thanks and acknowledgment to
Mike Newton for his contribution to this work.

CALL TO ARMS

Revolt and terror pay a price.
Order and law have a cost.
—Carl Sandburg,
The People, Yes

There *is* a price for terrorism in a civilized society. This time around, the men responsible are picking up the tab.
—Mack Bolan

To the memory of William Colby, retired director of
Central Intelligence and the man who kept the secrets.
Rest in peace.

1

The Everglades have hit hard times in the past few years: wildfires; a chronic water shortage that has jeopardized not only plants and wildlife, but the tourist industry, as well; cutbacks in Congress for the Parks Department; a freeze on adding animals to the endangered-species list; plane crashes that demanded earth-moving equipment and diversion of the normal water flow before equipment and remains could be retrieved.

But still, the swamp lives on.

One early explorer nicknamed it the River of Grass, and the name fit so well that it has stuck all these years. Vast portions of the Glades, when scrutinized by aerial reconnaissance—or even from the surface, in a skiff—have the appearance of a vast, impossibly neglected lawn, no water visible amid the cattails, reeds and grasses that deceive unwary travelers into believing they've discovered solid ground. Step from your skiff or skimmer, though, and you discover the mistake, swallowed by brackish water full of algae, moss and leeches that grow up to eighteen inches long. The water moccasins will probably ignore you if you don't disturb them while you're thrashing to the surface, but the great swamp's alligator population has exploded in the past two decades, under government protection, and there is a decent chance that some old bull will try you on for size.

The risks are worse at night. You lose your landmarks in the darkness, or they look entirely different, even if you find them with the spotlight mounted on your skiff. The swamp becomes an eerie constellation of fantastic lights: fireflies and other insects, phosphorescent plankton and the eyes of predators or scavengers who follow every move a stranger makes, in case the new arrival turns out to be food.

Mack Bolan didn't fear the swamp by day or night. He chose the darkness to conceal himself from human eyes and didn't use the outboard motor on the Zodiac inflatable boat to power him along. There would be time enough for noise and speed on his return, assuming he could reach the Zodiac, assuming it was still afloat.

Assuming he was still alive.

All great swamps have a smell about them, part of which is stagnant water, another part swamp gas. But mostly, what a person smells in a great swamp is death. From rotting vegetation, to the last remains of predators and prey, the swamp is one big waste-disposal unit. Nothing stops the process: drought, fire, flooding. The swamp is death—and life, as well, but it is death that lends its fragrance to the scene. If man bulldozed the Everglades and paved them over, the reek of death would still remain to haunt him.

The smell of death was nothing new to Bolan. He had smelled it in the swamps and jungles, in the desert and in cities where the most expensive air-conditioning couldn't compete with Mother Nature taking back her own. The smell didn't disturb him. Death was part of life and came to everyone in time. This night, with any luck at all, it would find someone else.

His enemies.

They waited for him in the midnight darkness, most of

them asleep by now—or so he hoped, at least. There would be sentries, but he was prepared to deal with them. The trick was getting close enough to use a knife, garrote or silenced pistol, when the smallest sound was carried by the night and echoed over water. If he wasn't very cautious, he could give himself away.

And that would be the end of Bolan's night probe, possibly his life. It took only one lookout with a steady hand and halfway decent weapon, one clean shot, to take him down. He wore a lightweight Kevlar vest beneath his camouflage fatigues, but it had mainly been designed for pistol rounds and shotgun pellets. Many rifle slugs could penetrate the body armor, if they didn't find the gap below each arm, and even if it worked, the material sheathed only his upper torso. There was still the head, both arms—with crucial arteries—and everything below the waist.

He wasn't bulletproof. He damn sure wasn't Superman. But Bolan knew what he was doing. He had skill, experience and motivation. He had scouted out his target in advance, with some assistance from surveillance satellites and topographic surveys.

Still…

All that was theory, background, homework. You could never really tell about a strike until the game was under way. Like now. So far, it felt all right, but anything could happen. The Executioner was prepared to bet his life that he could do the job.

In fact, he already had.

SWAMPS SUCKED, Virgil Blankenship thought.

It wasn't that he hated nature, but working in a place like the Everglades raised problems he had never thought of. And it wasn't just the water, which was rarely more than six feet deep no matter where you went and often barely deep enough to wet your socks if you were wearing low-topped shoes. No, sir.

The saw grass, as much as twelve feet tall in places, was sharp enough to shred fatigues and draw blood from the flesh beneath. It grew in clumps and rows that were nearly impossible to penetrate unless you spent a whole day sweating with machetes, clearing out a path. The grass put down its roots in peat and marl—a gummy mix of silt and clay—that measured ten or twelve yards deep in spots before you hit the bedrock limestone. Christ, the FAA lost *airliners* in there, and Blankenship himself had lost a pickup truck one August afternoon, when Tommy Binion got drunk and decided he'd drive into town. He missed the road, and while he scrambled clear before the truck went down, they never got the pickup back.

To Blankenship's way of thinking, it had been a poor trade.

One thing about the Glades, though: they supplied a fair amount of privacy. In fact, secret guerrilla armies had been training in the swamp for decades, going back to Ike's and JFK's adventure at the Bay of Pigs, on through the wars in Nicaragua and El Salvador, Honduras, Guatemala—hell, you name it. This was where the Seminoles played hide-and-seek with U.S. troops for years and finally fought them to a standstill, though they lost the rest of Florida while they hid out in the swamp. Today, aside from tourists, who were more or less confined to certain areas, you had drug labs and smugglers, gator poachers, secret graveyards nobody would ever find.

The Glades might suck in terms of comfort, but at least they were secure—or had been, anyway, until Chris Stone showed up. These days, with all the shit that had been going on, you couldn't be too sure of anything.

Blankenship was glad when Stone had left the camp at

sundown, heading for a night out in Miami. Both of them could use a break, the way they had been getting on each other's nerves, and it had been only two days. Stone acted as if he owned the place, as though he were God's man on the scene instead of someone who dropped in to bring bad news and hung around to make himself at home. And Blankenship had known the news already, most of it, which meant that Stone was basically deadweight, an extra mouth to feed.

The trouble with that was, he just might speak for Colonel Pike—if they could ever sort the pieces out from all the shit that had gone down in Idaho, and afterward in Baja. Blankenship had known some of the boys who bought it out west, and while he couldn't rightly say that all of them were friends, there was a kinship even so. They had been soldiers of the same cause, working for the same thing in the end.

Of course, the end came early to some, while others got to stick around awhile. And Blankenship, for his part, was in no rush to check out the afterlife.

Which helped explain why he had doubled the guard since Stone arrived and kicked morale into the crapper, just when Blankenship's people could have used a boost. The swamp got old, God knew, when you thought you were *winning*. And it got old that much faster when you knew your friends were out there in the real world, fighting for their lives and mostly losing when you couldn't do a thing to help.

He ordered himself to relax. They were all right where they were.

He hoped they were all right. If not, well, it would be a long swim to the nearest town of any consequence, where they could look for help or simply try to hide.

They had dry land, more or less, from weeks of dredging with equipment rented from a member of the KKK in Hialeah, and the buildings in the camp were elevated from the soggy ground on sawed-off telephone poles. Snakes and other creatures got underneath that way, and more than one of Blankenship's men had missed his footing in the dark to twist an ankle when he fell, but it still beat replacing rotten floorboards every month or two. As for the rest of it, the swamp had toughened up his people; there was no damn doubt about it.

He reckoned he had some of the best soldiers in the Paul Revere Militia, nationwide. Now he just hoped that Stone hadn't brought trouble upon them, when there were a thousand other places that he could have gone to hide. As for the captain's brilliant battle plan—

The shock of the explosion took his breath away, as if someone had punched him in the stomach when he wasn't looking, didn't have a chance to tighten up his abs and take it like a man. He swiveled toward the sound in time to see a fireball wafting from the farthest barracks on his left.

He vaulted from the platform of his quarters, moving out before a decent strategy could take shape in his mind, and all that he could think was that everything was going to hell.

BOLAN DIDN'T USE a timer on the C-4 plastique charge. Too many things could still go wrong, he realized, and a delay, even by seconds, could prove fatal to his timetable. As it was, he had the charges all in place, on the perimeter, before he made his way back to the starting point of his incursion, at the northwest corner of the camp.

He couldn't hear the numbers falling, in the sense that they were audible, like voices in his head, but Bolan felt time passing, in his pulse, with each breath he drew. It

wasn't that he had a deadline or a hostage to be rescued—
not this time, at least—but combat was a lot like comedy:
timing was everything, and the ideal performance called
for him to kill his audience. A stand-up comic used that
line with tongue in cheek, of course, but Bolan took it
literally.

Time to rock.

He scanned the camp again, picking out the sentries
and a soldier coming back from the latrine, away to Bolan's right. He had no doubt that there were others still
awake, and that was fine. As for the soldiers who were
sleeping now, he meant to wake them up—before he put
them back to sleep forever.

Go!

He found the detonator on his combat harness, nestled
close beside a fragmentation grenade, the plastic box a
trifle smaller than a pack of cigarettes. Up close, it looked
a little like a pocket calculator, with a power switch to
turn it on, a keypad for selection of specific charges by
their number—if they weren't required to blow as one—
and the red button that would beam a signal to begin the
light show. Bolan had decided on selective detonation,
charges one through seven, and he punched a button for
the fifth one, directly opposite his hiding place, some forty
yards across the camp. He closed his eyes to help preserve
his night vision, and thumbed the scarlet button.

The shock wave reached the Executioner where he huddled beneath one of the huts on stilts, and he felt the hot
breath of the fireball on his face. Someone was screaming,
and other voices joined in seconds later, cursing, shouting
questions, one or two attempting to bring order out of
sudden chaos, barking orders at the men.

Bolan keyed another charge, sixty yards off to his left,
where two Jeeps and a pickup truck were parked under

camo netting. He had gooped the middle vehicle and trusted flying, flaming gasoline to do the rest, a fiery beacon rising in the pitch-dark of the Everglades. The camo net caught fire above the burning vehicles and started to unravel like a spiderweb in pelting rain.

His enemies were everywhere, some of them milling in the center of the compound now, while others ran to pre-assigned positions, sentries pulling in from farther out to find out what was going down. Bolan unslung his M-16, made heavier than usual by the 40-mm M-203 launcher slung beneath its barrel, and prepared to meet his prey.

Fish in a barrel, Bolan told himself, and knew before the thought took shape that it was never all that easy. Fish didn't shoot back, for one thing, and this "barrel" was the home team's turf, their training ground. He didn't have a lock on victory, by any means, and the advantage of surprise was only that—an advantage, not a guarantee.

He duck-walked out of hiding, still in shadow, though the firelight served to give the camp illumination it had lacked before. His targets cast long shadows in front of them, men running here and there, all yammering at once. Nobody was shooting yet, and while that was a bit of a surprise, he knew exactly how to deal with it.

Two moving targets came at Bolan from his right, not charging him, not even knowing who or what he was, just making tracks. Before they had a chance to recognize their peril, file the information and respond effectively, he had them covered with the M-16, his finger taking up the rifle's trigger slack. A burst of 5.56 mm projectiles cut through both men where they stood and slammed them over backward to the sodden ground.

The sound of automatic gunfire, coming close behind the two explosions, told his enemies that there would be no rational, safe explanation for chaos that surrounded them. They were already paranoid, conditioned to believe that most Americans were enemies of theirs—depending on their race, religion, politics, whatever—and that any combination of those several hundred million enemies might constitute a clear and present danger to their lives at any time. The blacks might send a raiding party out to hunt them in the Glades, or crack Israeli-trained commandos might be fielded by the Jews. Hell, it could even be the FBI or ATF, assigned by ZOG—the Zionist Occupational Government in Washington, D.C.—to hound the last *real* patriots into their graves.

Bolan was moving by the time his first two kills collapsed in front of him. Backtracking toward the bungalow where he had hidden when he triggered the explosions, he circled around behind it, moving like the shadow of a night-prowler. A young man nearly ran into him, naked to the waist and barefoot, wearing nothing but fatigue pants, carrying a Ruger Mini-14 in his hands.

"What's hap—?"

The butt of Bolan's M-16 lashed out and caught him on the left side of his face before he could complete the question, slamming him sideways, still alive as he went down but long past fighting. Bolan left him where he lay, not worth a bullet. By the time he came back to his senses—*if* he did—the battle should be over.

Go! Go! Go!

He keyed another blast, thirty yards behind him, and kept on running, seeking targets. It was all about momentum now, taking advantage of his lead, and anything that moved was Bolan's prey.

BOB SACKETT WAS a gung ho kind of soldier. He had never made it in the real Army, what with the psychological exams and all, but he had grown up lusting for a uniform, a chance to fight his country's enemies. His brother had been killed in Desert Storm, and Sackett had been jealous of him, standing there at graveside while the soldiers in their best dress uniforms removed Old Glory from his coffin, folded it just so and gave it to his mother as if it were some kind of door prize.

Not that Sackett was anxious to get killed, but that was what a soldier risked when he put on the uniform, picked up the gun. Death was a measure of devotion to the cause, a way—the number-one way, absolutely—to let everybody know exactly where you stood.

Sackett had work to do, the burden of a righteous duty balanced on his shoulders and supported by the sergeant's stripes that graced his sleeve. He was a noncom in the Paul Revere Militia, had been for the past three months. Authority hadn't gone to his head—at least, he didn't think it had—but rather, it had filled him with a new sense of responsibility.

He grabbed the mini-Uzi from his makeshift nightstand, nothing but a plastic crate for milk jugs standing on one end, a bent nail holding it against the clapboard wall, to stop it turning over accidentally. It wasn't Sackett's night on duty, and he had been sleeping in his undershorts when an explosion rocked the camp, followed immediately by another, then a burst of automatic gunfire. That spelled trouble, which in turn spelled action and a chance for Sackett to really prove himself.

He had never actually killed a man before, although he had participated in some drive-bys in Nevada, where he used to live, a little welcome party for the Cubans and Vietnamese who kept confusing Vegas with their native land. Sackett had always wanted to kill someone, though, and now, with all the training he had had, it looked as if he would get his chance.

Emerging from his quarters, he found chaos in the camp. The sentries obviously didn't have a clue as to the location of the intruders. From what he saw, they couldn't even make up their minds as to whether they should dig in, sweep the camp's perimeter or simply chase the sounds of combat as they moved around the compound. They seemed hopelessly disorganized, and while he wanted to take charge of them, the sergeant knew it would be worth his stripes—if not his life—to usurp Virgil Blankenship's authority.

He had to find the captain, find out what he wanted him to do. If Blankenship was dead or removed from his command, that would mean Sackett was in charge, but until that happened, he was still a sergeant. Taking orders was a major part of every day, and while he used to rankle at authority, Sackett had learned to live with it, all for the good of America.

He started searching for the captain, pausing to check bodies when he saw one, roll the dead man over, checking faces. Sackett recognized all of them, soldiers from the camp, some of them friends, all wasted now. But Blankenship wasn't among them, and he kept on searching, one eye peeled for any opportunity to nail one of the enemy.

The way he found the captain was an accident, a total fluke. Sackett was moving toward the mess hall, passing by one of the bungalows on stilts, when yet another blast went off behind him, knocking Sackett to all fours. He scrabbled for the mini-Uzi, got it back and was about to rise when he glanced over to his right and found the camp commander staring at him, bug-eyed, from the crawl space underneath the bungalow.

"Captain?" He still couldn't believe it, despite the evidence. Why wasn't Blankenship out in the middle of the action, rallying his men? Was he afraid?

"Sackett." Blankenship spoke with a tremor in his voice, as if he were standing in the middle of a blizzard with no coat to keep him warm.

"What's going on, sir?" Sackett was frightened of the answer he might get, a little angry to see Blankenship this way, determined more than ever not to let his own emotions get the best of him.

"We need to get the men together," Blankenship replied, but made no move to act upon his words.

"Yes, sir."

"You...you handle that, now, will you, son?"

The next thing after shock and anger was disgust, with just enough pity thrown in to keep him from responding with a long string of obscenities. Blankenship wasn't fit to lead the troops, but he still had the captain's bars.

"I'll try and find Lieutenant James," Sackett said, forgetting to salute as he scrambled to his feet.

"Too late," the captain called to him. "He's dead. I found him by the motor pool."

God*damn!* No wonder the old man was nervous. Still, he should have more guts than to hide because one man got killed, no matter that they had been friends from junior high or something.

"I'll take care of it."

IT TOOK A KEEN, almost detached mind to keep track of the charges he had fired and those that remained while he was fighting for his life. Bolan released the trigger of his M-16 and watched a man topple over dead, blood spilling from the three holes in his chest. He swiftly took stock of his whereabouts, enough to plot the three remaining charges in his mind.

To hell with it.

He blew them all at once and staggered slightly as the

charges detonated together, two off on his right, the third one to his left. The noise was brutal, battering his eardrums even with the plastic shooting plugs he wore. He saw a body airborne, tumbling like an acrobat, except that acrobats didn't set themselves on fire before they launched into their next routines. The dead man landed on his back, the impact snuffing out most of the flames.

Bolan ignored the smoking corpse and concentrated on the living. His reconnaissance had led him to believe that thirty-five or forty would-be soldiers occupied the outpost in the Everglades, and while he couldn't say how many had been taken out by the charges he had detonated, there were still enough of them around to make things dangerous.

He kept an eye out for Chris Stone, unhappy that he had been forced to make his move without a final confirmation that the primary target was on-site, but he was in the middle of it now, with nothing to be gained from second-guessing and regret. He had to deal with those in front of him, and never let his guard down for a moment.

The Executioner emptied the last rounds from his M-16's magazine into a runner on his left, and watched the man sprawl on his face. Reloading as he put the corpse behind him, Bolan focused on the prospect of a more methodical search, some method that would let him sweep the camp, find Stone if he was hiding there, determine if he had slipped through the net.

And if he missed his man, what then?

Start over.

Giving up wasn't a part of Bolan's strategy for handling any problem. He might be forced to retreat from time to time, but he would always come back swinging until his enemies had been reduced and neutralized.

A swarm of bullets crackled overhead. He spun in the

direction of the gunfire, bringing up his weapon, searching out the threat. Two young militiamen were advancing on him, their faces twisted into masks of rage or panic, their first rounds wasted in the shock of picking out an enemy. He couldn't count on either one of them repeating the mistake.

The Executioner moved out to meet their guns.

2

It seemed to take forever, but Blankenship could feel it when the tide of battle changed. There was nothing that he could put his finger on, but there was something. Even though his men were catching hell, getting their asses kicked, he recognized the change when it arrived.

And Blankenship decided that they might still have a chance.

He knew what Sackett thought of him. It had been written on the sergeant's face, as plain as day, and that was fine. Just so the little bastard kept it to himself and didn't get some bright idea that he could steal the show, take over from the man whom Ralph Pike had chosen to command the Paul Revere Militia in the Sunshine State. If Blankenship even thought that kind of move was coming at him, he would have to take dramatic steps to head it off. But at the moment, he had other, more important problems on his hands.

Like how to keep his Everglades command from being slaughtered while he was hiding from the enemy as if he were a frightened child.

It wasn't something he could easily explain, the sudden fear that had possessed him, driving him to cover like a green recruit his first time under fire. The explanation didn't really matter, anyway. It was enough that he had been discovered, that the word would get around. Enough to know that if he didn't move damn quick, do something to redeem himself in Sackett's eyes, there would eventually be more hurt coming down on him than he could handle.

He blamed Chris Stone. The bastard had been running out on fights the past two weeks, and now he wasn't even here to face the music when his enemies came looking for him. Blankenship had tried to work it out, and there was just no other explanation for the sudden holocaust that had descended on his camp. It was Stone's fault.

Reluctantly, still trembling, Blankenship crawled out from underneath the bungalow and stood, shoulders hunched, as if he knew a bullet was about to slam between them. The sounds of combat were now concentrated at the northwest corner of the camp, still brisk and loud, but not as all-encompassing as they had been mere heartbeats earlier.

Were the attackers pulling out? Had something spooked them? Were they losing men and running out of time? It pleased Blankenship to think so, but he couldn't know for sure. Not that it mattered in the last analysis. His men were mostly rushing off in that direction, some of them blood smeared and hobbling, wounded, wanting to be in the middle of the action while it lasted. They put Blankenship to shame, and thereby stiffened his resolve to act.

Even as he focused on the simple act of walking, he could hear the gunfire fading off into the swamp. Some kind of a retreat was in progress, thank God, while he still had sufficient numbers to defend the camp against a second rush if it was necessary.

Could it be a trap?

He spun around and scanned the darkness at his back, eyes tearing from the smoke and stench of burning flesh. If there were raiders out there, watching from the swamp, they didn't seem in any hurry to attack. He put the problem out of mind and turned back toward his men, picked up his pace and drew his pistol as he closed the gap between them. Hell, he might as well appear as if he had participated in the fight.

Sackett stepped out to meet him as he neared the group of soldiers, several others close behind the sergeant, watching Blankenship. Had the sergeant already informed them of his cowardice? It seemed unlikely, but he had to take the chance.

"They took off through the swamp," the sergeant said. "A couple of the fellas saw them go."

"Saw *one* go," someone in the ranks corrected him.

"One man?" Blankenship asked. It seemed impossible, but Stone had said...

"We can't be sure," Sackett replied. "Anyway, they don't have much of a head start. We should go after them."

It wasn't such a brilliant plan, Blankenship thought, allowing for the darkness, snakes and gators, not to mention that they didn't have a clue how many adversaries they were facing. Still, if he refused, it might give Sackett the opening he needed, something he could use as concrete evidence of his superior's failure as a leader.

"Right," he said, already knowing that it was a bad idea. "Pick out your people, Sergeant. Bring me a survivor if you can."

"You won't be coming, sir?" There was an undertone to Sackett's question, nothing you could single out as insubordinate, but getting there.

"Somebody has to tend the wounded," Blankenship replied, and gripped his pistol tightly, ready if the sergeant tried to call him on it, make some kind of stink.

But Sackett only smiled and snapped him a salute of sorts. "Yes, sir," he said. "We'll get right on it."

As Sackett started calling off the names of soldiers for his chase team, Blankenship was turning back to scan the wreckage of his camp. They could save some of it, at least, but it wouldn't be easy. They would all feel better once the man or men responsible for this was punished. Better yet, if Sackett brought one back for questioning...

And if the sergeant had a little accident, while he was slogging through the swamp, why, that would be a crying shame.

BOLAN HAD FELT the mission going sour on him when he realized that there were more guns in the camp than he had estimated. Whether Stone had called for reinforcements or the men were simply gathered for a special training exercise, he had no way of knowing, and it made no difference to him either way. He could have lingered in the camp and tried to shoot it out with them, but in the seeming absence of the one man he had come to kill, it was a risky waste of time.

But pulling back involved some hazards all its own. The swamp was unforgiving with a visitor who made mistakes, and haste on unfamiliar ground—or water—was the surest way to make an error. Bolan's need for speed could get him killed as quickly by the perils of the swamp as any hesitation on his part could get him shot by those pursuing him.

And there could be no doubt that they were after him. He heard them coming, airboats revving up their giant fans, their spotlights burning tunnels through the darkness, searching for him. Gunners would be waiting for a target to appear, and they would have the primary advantage if they spotted Bolan while he was on foot. They had him beaten with their speed, but he wasn't finished yet.

He slogged through waist-deep water, thankful that it wasn't deeper, feeling mud and peat suck at his combat boots with every step he took. He held his M-16/M-203 above the water, even though he knew the weapon could survive a dunking. There was no point taking chances if he could avoid it, when his life was riding on the function of his battle gear. As long as he could keep his weapons reasonably dry, so much the better. And when it was time for him to rock—

A searchlight fell across him, swept away, then hesitated, coming back. Before the beam could reacquire its target, he was moving, sloshing through the water, saw grass slashing at him as he drove for the cover of a giant cypress tree. It wasn't much, but any cover at the moment was a great deal better than a stand in plain sight of his enemies.

Long tails of Spanish moss hung from the cypress branches overhead like veils of moldy and moth-eaten lace. His camouflage fatigues and war paint blended nicely with the background, though he couldn't count on being overlooked if they surrounded him and really used the spotlights, banishing the shadows that protected him. Before things went that far, Bolan thought, he would have to make his move.

And make it count.

He heard the airboats coming for him, two of them at least. More engine sounds off in the distance told him these weren't the only searchers looking for him. Hasty mental calculations told him that each standard airboat would accommodate one pilot and anywhere from four to half a dozen passengers, depending on how they were packed aboard. Right now, Bolan was less concerned with any formal head count than with taking out his adversaries' means of transportation. Once the hunters were on foot, it would become a simple numbers game, and the Executioner was prepared to match his own survival skills against these shooters any day.

He double-checked the M-203 launcher, making sure that it was loaded with a high-explosive round. The 40 mm HE loads weren't considered antipersonnel munitions in the strictest sense, as they provided nothing in the way of major shrapnel, but he thought they should do for the job he had in mind. The weapon boasted an effective range of some 400 meters, but he planned on working much closer than that, which meant that Bolan needed pinpoint timing, both to nail his target and to keep himself from being caught up in the blast.

He waited, trying to gauge the distance of the airboats by their engine noise and the voices of their gunners shouting questions back and forth. They seemed uncertain as to whether one of them had spotted anything or not, arguing whether someone known as Bubba was an idiot or simply blind. Somebody finally snapped at them to knock it off, and Bolan lost their voices as the airboats jockeyed for position, coming up on either side of him.

Which way to go with the grenade? It seemed to make no difference, left or right, and Bolan dared not risk a glance to see if one boat might be marginally closer than the other. Make it the left, then, Bolan decided on a mental coin toss.

He guessed the distance, judging from experience and his surroundings, counting down from five. On *four*, he had his finger on the M-203's trigger, with the weapon's stock tucked well into his armpit, braced against his ribs. *Three* found him with his legs bent slightly, gaining leverage, testing his boots to be sure they would lift clear of the muck when it was time for him to move. On *two*, he started edging to his left, the dank moss brushing at his face like witch's hair. Some kind of insect scuttled awkwardly across his cheek and down inside his collar. Bolan let it go and made his turn on *one*.

He was stepping clear on *zero*, squinting in the glare of searchlights, squeezing off his HE round before the hunters on the airboat he had chosen realized that they were really seeing movement in the dark, before they had a chance to recognize the shadow with a human form and face. Somebody opened fire, but he was ducking backward out of range, and then all hell broke loose.

The night was suddenly on fire, and angry voices were replaced by wailing screams.

SACKETT WINCED at the explosion, coming eighty yards or so off to his left. He had deliberately spread out the airboats because he didn't have a clue how many shooters he was looking for, what sort of hardware they were packing or what kind of transportation they might have. The best way to catch up with them, in Sackett's view, was with a broad sweep, some two hundred yards across, to scour the swamp, run out a couple miles at speed, then double back and close it up to look for any stragglers they had missed. It might not be a perfect plan, but it was all he could come up with in a hurry, and he absolutely refused to show an indecisive face before his men.

That kind of thinking was what made him leadership material. It was responsible for his promotion in the Paul Revere Militia, and he knew that it would serve him even better in the ASA—American Secret Army—when things got rolling and their program started catching on.

Sackett brought his mind back to the search, and he was just about to have his pilot nudge the airboat to his left, to check some hummocks where the saw grass was unusually dense and tall, when the explosion told him they had contact.

"Over there!" he shouted, pointing to the fireball that resembled nothing so much as a giant flower sculpted out of neon. "Knock on it!"

"I'm there," the pilot told him, hauling on the airboat's rudder, opening the throttle until they were skimming across the surface of the water. In their wake, an eight-foot swath of saw grass, flattened by the airboat's hull, sprang back to life once they had passed.

Sackett had traded in his mini-Uzi for an AR-15 rifle, the civilian version of the M-16, illegally converted to full-auto by a neo-Nazi gunsmith in Fort Lauderdale. The guy was as crazy as a bedbug when it came to Jews, but he could tune a weapon like some kind of virtuoso working on a Stradivarius. His pieces also had a lifetime guarantee for normal wear and tear: if anything broke down or jammed in standard operating situations, with a decent load, the gunsmith told his outlaw customers that he would make himself available to take a bullet in the head, their call.

You didn't get that kind of pride in modern craftsmen nowadays.

Sackett and his companions had been running in the middle of the search line, and he grabbed his walkie-talkie, shouting for the last two boats to join him just in case they contrived to miss the fireworks show. Both pilots snapped acknowledgment, and Sackett didn't bother looking back to find their searchlights, trusting them to do as they were told.

Besides, ground zero was no more than forty yards in front of him by then, and he was concentrating on the burning wreckage of the airboat, watching as its sister craft made a three-sixty in the water, kicking up a wall of murky foam, and swung back toward a giant cypress frozen in its searchlight beam. Sackett was studying the tree, looking for anything to indicate the presence of an enemy, and still he almost missed it when the second high-explosive round was fired. There was a muffled *bonk*ing sound, no muzzle-flash, and then he saw the racing airboat rear back on its tail, a spout of mingled flame and water erupting from beneath its bow.

Sackett stood gaping as the airboat's deck was cleared, three bodies splashing down as their conveyance kept on going, the big fan biting saw grass, churning up the muddy water as it slipped below the surface. A second later, when the engine died, the airboat toppled over on one side and came to rest in water three or four feet deep, its starboard side wedged in the muck.

He turned back toward the cypress and was just in time to see a man-shaped shadow move behind the veil of Spanish moss, an orange light winking at him. *Muzzle-flashes!*

"Jesus! Left! Go left!"

The airboat swung hard left, and Sackett lost his footing. A moment later, he was airborne, plummeting toward splashdown in the swamp.

THE OTHER AIRBOATS WERE converging on him when he fired the second HE round, and Bolan had a fleeting opportunity to count the searchlights. Four were all that he could see, which meant something between a dozen guns and twenty-five, depending on their loads. Two of the boats were closer than the second pair, which told him he couldn't afford to wait for all of them to reach him, or the shooters in the first two boats would have him cold.

It took only a heartbeat to reload the launcher as he

ducked back under cover, circling toward the far side of
the massive cypress bole. The hunters in the lead weren't
firing yet, still waiting for a solid target, and he knew he
would have two or three clear seconds, once he made his
move into the lights, before they could identify him as a
human, swing around their guns and open fire.

Three seconds was a lifetime in the hellgrounds.

Bolan made his move, the water swirling darkly at his
waist, muck clutching at his boots. He came around the
cypress bole and squinted in the closest searchlight's
glare, his weapon leveled from the waist. Behind it, there
were only silhouettes in human form, one of them certainly the pilot on his high seat, with the tall cage of the
airboat's giant fan behind him. Bolan stood his ground
and fired off half a magazine, grinning in satisfaction as
the searchlight blew. Somebody on the deck shouted for
the pilot to go left, the airboat veering, slicing through the
saw grass. As he stepped back under cover, Bolan thought
he saw one of the passengers go overboard, a miserable
dive that wouldn't win him any points at all.

The airboat he had blinded kept on going, and the other
three were drawing closer by the heartbeat, searchlights
blazing through the murky darkness of the swamp. The
sound reminded him of buzz saws, but without the high-
pitched whine that told you when a blade bit into wood.

He would assume the hunters had some method of com-
munication, though they probably wouldn't have needed
it to home in on the twin blasts of his HE rounds, and
now his automatic-rifle fire. The M-16 had no suppressor
on its muzzle, and while it wasn't the loudest weapon in
the world, it wouldn't pass for silent in the late-night still-
ness of the Everglades.

And it *was* still, he realized. The background music of
night birds and insects had evaporated when the airboats

came, completely silenced by the sounds of combat. When the killing work was done, he knew, the swamp would soon come back to life, but in the meantime, live-in predators and prey alike would be his audience, observing from a cautious distance while men hunted one another in the Glades.

One of the airboats hurtled past his shelter, leaving saw grass flattened in its wake, and made a broad U-turn to double back. For all its speed and shallow draft, the boat was basically a wide raft with a fan attached in back, and it required some room in which to turn. Before the pilot had completed his maneuver, Bolan had his target zeroed in, the M-16's stock braced against his shoulder as his index finger found the trigger of the M-203 launcher.

There was no recoil worth considering, as the propellant charge dispatched another HE round from thirty yards. It landed in the pilot's lap, or near enough to vault him from his perch when it exploded, someone screaming from the stricken vessel as his body somersaulted through a cloud of smoke and flame. The gunners dived or fell away to either side, and Bolan counted two of them before the airboat's fuel tank blew, sending another fireball wafting toward the treetops.

He would have to think about the gunmen in the water after he had taken care of all the airboats. If he managed to survive that long, it should be relatively simple taking out the stragglers, shaken as they were, some of them wounded, possibly disarmed. But while they still had lights and speed...

Three boats remained, two with searchlights, but the one he had already blinded was the nearest to where Bolan stood, its engine throttled back and idling as it drifted through the saw grass. The Executioner leaned around the tree and took advantage of the searchlights on the other boats to scan its deck.

He spotted two men still aboard, one sprawled beneath the pilot's elevated seat, the other stepping past him, mounting to the perch as Bolan watched, and reaching for the controls. Another moment, if he knew the drill, and he could have the airboat moving, bring it back around and make another run at Bolan from his flank.

Or maybe not.

The shot was nothing, fifty feet or less, with lights approaching rapidly to frame his target in the rifle sights. It was the kind of shooting he had done so much of back in Southeast Asia, more or less, except for shorter range and the nationality of the selected target. The soldier set the rifle's fire-selector switch for semiauto, stroked the trigger once and watched his mark sprawl sideways, lurching from the pilot's seat to form a second boneless lump upon the deck.

And that left two boats.

He fed the M-16 another magazine to make sure it was ready for the action, and returned the switch to its full-auto setting. Any second now, and he would have an airboat rushing past on either side. It would be down to speed, efficiency and skill.

The same as always.

He braced himself and took a deep breath, getting ready for the kill.

SACKETT WAS BLEEDING when he burst up through the scummy surface of the water, slashed by saw grass on his face and scalp when he was pitched into the swamp. He sucked in air and tasted pond scum in his mouth, spit some of it away and wound up gagging.

Sackett was in the water, he was bleeding and there

wasn't one damn thing that he could do about it at the moment. If a gator came along and bagged him, he was dead, but in the meantime, he had more immediate concerns.

He checked himself, deciding that the bullets had to have missed him. That had been a lucky break, even considering his tumble from the airboat. By the time he wobbled through a full one-eighty, he could see the boat that threw him, sitting seventy or eighty feet away, its engine idling, with what looked to be a pair of dead men lying on the deck. The only reason he could see their bodies was because of the searchlights!

He turned back toward the last two airboats, nearly panicked as he saw them gaining on him, then decided they would miss him if both pilots held their present courses, running twenty-five or thirty feet apart. No sweat.

That was before they thundered past him, one on either side, their wakes colliding in the middle to create a swell of stinking, stagnant water just where Sackett was standing, ankle-deep in peat and fighting for his balance. Scummy water swamped him, the saw grass whipping back and forth around him like a hedge of razor wire lashed by a windstorm.

He lost his footing, slid beneath the surface once again, then fought his way back to the air. Some of the roaring in his ears was blood inside his veins, he knew, but most of it was gunfire, mixed with noise from racing engines as the airboats went on the attack. He turned in an attempt to follow them, aware that he had lost his rifle when he went into the drink. That left a pistol on his belt, below the waterline, assuming it would even fire.

He was fumbling with his holster when the airboat on his right exploded. They were charging toward that cypress, where the gunman had emerged to fire on his boat moments earlier, and then the engine or the fuel tank seemed to detonate, flinging burning gas and shrapnel off in all directions.

Gasoline was burning on the surface of the water now, distorting Sackett's vision, but he still saw well enough to spot the target—was it just one man?—as he turned back to bring the other airboat under fire. He carried a bulky weapon, a loaded M-16, and the launcher would explain how he was blasting boats out of the water as if there was nothing to it.

Sackett saw the muzzle-flashes from his adversary's weapon lancing toward the final airboat. Someone on the deck was firing back at him and missing by a good two yards in the excitement. Sackett felt like shouting for them to get the bastard, but he kept his mouth shut, reckoning that it was smarter not to let the shooter know exactly where he was.

And in another moment, he was glad, when one of the militiamen took a burst square in the chest and vaulted backward, slamming into his companion. Both men went sprawling, while the pilot soaked up two or three rounds on his own. The way the bullets took him, he slumped forward, covering the throttle, and the airboat kept on going at full speed until it met another giant cypress tree head-on.

Sackett didn't have to ponder on the source of that explosion. The airboat buckled up like an accordion, the big fan whirring, driving forward even after there was nowhere left to go. Then it flew apart and sent its great blades twanging off across the swamp.

And for the first time, Sackett understood exactly why his captain had been hiding underneath the bungalow on stilts back at the camp instead of getting out and hunting for the enemy. Scared shitless you could call it, if you wanted to, and that was fine.

He left his pistol where it was, and crouched so just his head was clear. The water lapping underneath his chin, he turned around, duck-walking back toward camp. The saw grass cut him, but he didn't let it slow him. He was alive, and that was all that mattered.

If the gators missed him, heading back to camp, Sackett decided he would have to view old Virgil with a more forgiving eye. And maybe he could use a long vacation.

Why not?

3

Bolan had been a long time getting to the Everglades. His mission had begun almost a month before, when he had gone along with Hal Brognola's plan to light a fire beneath the Paul Revere Militia, which was linked to several daring robberies and acts of right-wing terrorism in the western half of the United States. The group's agenda was essentially identical to that of several hundred other fringe groups in America—that is to say, a frantic, sometimes paranoid pursuit of "good old days" that never were— but this particular organization had an edge over the rest.

Specifically its leaders—Colonel Ralph Pike and his second-in-command, Chris Stone—were hard-core military veterans who had learned their craft the hard way, fighting for America on foreign soil before they came around to thinking that they should be fighting *in* America against the very government they once had taken oaths to serve. In Pike's case, it had been a case of disillusionment that followed Vietnam and the American decline from a respected superpower to a nation with a trillion-dollar deficit and a history of being pushed around, insulted and reviled by small-time dictators from Nicaragua to the Middle East. Stone had been taught to favor military-style solutions to most problems, and he brought that ethic to the Paul Reveres, recruiting men who ranged from ethical conservatives to crackpot racists hoping they could light the fuse to Armageddon.

Stone was something else. Another fighting man who had survived his share of combat zones while serving in the army, he had shifted to a mercenary life-style in pursuit of profit and continued doing what he had always done best, putting those skills the government had taught him on the open market. He would work for anyone, or so it seemed, and the assumption was that Pike and company had come in with the high bid for his services before he deigned to join the Paul Revere Militia as Pike's second-in-command, with special emphasis on training and devising strategy. The move to robbery and acts of terrorism may not have been Stone's idea, but the provision of his expertise was clearly a facilitating factor in the violence traced to members of the Paul Reveres.

Bolan had infiltrated the militia headquarters in Idaho, and after frustrating one of their raids, was poised to wreak grim judgment on the leadership and major strike teams when he was distracted by a lady Fed named Ginger Ross. She was an agent of the ATF, still chasing justice in the disappearance of her partner, who had vanished on a mission similar to Bolan's, some weeks earlier. Instead of backing off and following the orders of her supervisors, she had tried to play the game alone and wound up as a hostage of the Paul Revere Militia, marked for rough interrogation and eventual elimination by Chris Stone.

Bolan had tried to save the woman with a premature assault on the militia headquarters, which left Pike paralyzed and several dozen of his "soldiers" dead or fleeing for their lives. Bolan had failed to liberate the hostage, though, and Stone slipped away with Ross still in tow. Stone's trail led all the way to Baja California, where he had secured a temporary refuge with the members of a strange, militia-linked religious cult, and Bolan found him there. Despite involvement of the local *federales* in a network of corruption that included smuggling arms across the U.S. border, Bolan had successfully extracted Ginger Ross...but Stone had given him the slip a second time.

And run to Florida, as Bolan soon found out, where the militia was reportedly connected to a larger "patriotic" network, several right-wing, racist, neo-Nazi groups collaborating under the umbrella of an outfit they called the American Secret Army. Virgil Blankenship's militia wing was the hard core of ASA, but he wasn't alone. From all appearances, Chris Stone had found himself a halfway decent hiding place. Most searchers would have come up empty, frustrated by the determined wall of silence a collection of fanatics had erected to defend themselves from prosecution on a list of heavy charges that included arson, robbery, extortion, gunrunning and homicide.

But then again, most searchers weren't Mack Bolan. They were bound by rules of evidence and constitutional provisions that allowed suspected criminals to choose when they would talk, with whom and what they would discuss. All recent presidential-campaign promises aside, the justice system still leaned heavily in favor of defendants, and it always would. With the memory of British kangaroo courts fresh in mind, the Founding Fathers had designed it that way to minimize injustice, and you couldn't fault George Washington or Ben Franklin for the fact that they weren't clairvoyant, able to predict an age of drug wars, vicious sex crimes, random murder and the growth of worldwide syndicates devoted solely to the furtherance of evil deeds. It would have been like flashing back to Genesis and asking Adam to predict cruise missiles.

Unlike the Feds, local cops and prosecutors, though,

there were no rules to bind the Executioner, determine where he went or how he handled suspects as he carried out his duty. *He* made up the rules up as he went along, and number one was always simple: get results. Beyond that, Bolan wouldn't kill police in any circumstances, and he did his best to keep all innocent civilians from the line of fire. Within those broad parameters, the gloves were off, and those he hunted could expect the same degree of mercy they had shown to victims all their lives.

Precisely none.

His action in the Everglades had been a decent start, but Bolan still wished that he had been able to locate Stone and wrap it up. Most of his missions were completed in a day or two, a week at the outside, but this one felt as if it had begun to get away from him. When he lay down at night to snatch an hour or two of sleep, he dreamed about Stone dodging him across the surface of a giant globe, hopping from town to town, one country to the next, from continent to continent, while Bolan slogged along behind him, never getting close enough to make the final tag.

And he woke up each time with new determination to succeed, to make *this* killing ground the mercenary's last arena. There were no distractions this time. Ginger Ross was still out west somewhere, recovering from wounds sustained in Baja, and her supervisors wouldn't let her slip away from them again. This time, it would be Stone and Bolan.

But he knew that it wouldn't be one-on-one. Not even close.

There was a "secret" army waiting for him in the Sunshine State, and Stone had glimpsed him back in Baja long enough to know whom he was dealing with, at least in terms of physical description.

Nothing ever went the easy way, it seemed, in Bolan's war. But he was in for the duration, and he wasn't backing down. He had a job to do.

"I'M TELLING YOU," Virgil Blankenship said, "I don't know who the hell it was, okay? I don't know who, how many, anything about it. You're the expert, right? I mean, these bastards have been chasing you all over hell's half acre, right?"

Chris Stone was glaring at him, sitting with his back against the wall in a corner booth at a fast-food restaurant in Miami Springs. His face was pallid, with little spots of angry color showing on both cheeks, and Blankenship thought he had to be chewing on his tongue the way his jaw muscles kept clenching and relaxing.

"Well?" Blankenship demanded. "You going to say something or not? You dumped this shit in my lap, now you're clamming up on me? That's great!"

"I'm thinking, dammit!" Stone replied. "And keep your voice down, will you?"

Blankenship gave the angry glare right back to Stone. The more he saw of this one, now that Pike was out of it, the less he liked what he was seeing. He was on the verge of asking for a written order from the colonel, signed before he got injured in Idaho, that would require him to obey Stone's dictates. That could lead to trouble, and Blankenship wasn't about to do it here, at breakfast, but he would bide his time, get Stone in a position where he was surrounded, cornered.

"I'm waiting," Blankenship told his nominal superior.

"All right," Stone said. "I may know who your shooter is."

"My shooter? Like you're saying one guy did all that last night?"

"Why not?" Stone asked. His voice was calm now, no more angry color in his face.

"I got a man who contradicts you. He chased the hit team in the Glades last night, while I was picking up the pieces at the compound. He went in with six airboats and eighteen men, came back alone and walking. The way he tells it, there were six or seven guns at least, some kind of ambush, with grenades and shit."

"And he's the only one who made it out alive?" Stone almost seemed amused at that. "You grilled him thoroughly, I guess."

"I did. And I believe him."

"Suit yourself," Stone said. "All I can say is what went down in Idaho and Baja. First, we had the new guy—Mike Belasko, he called himself. I didn't think about him when it hit the fan in Idaho. That's my mistake, and I admit it, but I figured he was dead or running. Then in Baja, there he was, all painted up and carrying enough hardware to sweep Beirut, and he was taking out *my* men."

"Missed you, though," Blankenship couldn't resist observing.

"That was luck as much as anything."

"You didn't take him out, though, when you had the chance."

"Shit happens," the mercenary said. "Like tonight."

Now Blankenship felt color warming *his* cheeks. "The difference is," he said, "this shit was trucked in from the outside world and dumped on me, no fault of mine. Maybe I have to help you shovel it, okay. But I don't have to like it. And I can't do anything as long as you're still keeping secrets, playing games."

"Okay, that's fair," Stone said, but something in his eyes seemed shifty.

"I'm listening," Blankenship prompted.

"I don't have much," Stone told him. "Colonel Pike ran a background check, through channels, and it came back clean. This guy—call him Belasko for the sake of argument—had done some minor time for weapons, nothing that would raise a flag. His paperwork was in the system, like it should be if he was legit. We got a look inside his military record and the prison file. Records don't read the mind, but there was nothing on the books to contradict what he was saying, and we took him on a raid."

"The one in Colorado," Blankenship replied.

"That's right."

"The one where you were ambushed by the Feds, as I recall."

"That's right," Stone said again. "I'm way ahead of you. We looked at everybody on the strike team—everybody who survived—and that included Belasko."

"So?"

"So it came down to someone else. You ever meet Lou Doyle?"

"One time, I think. Seemed like an asshole."

"That's the guy," Stone said. "Belasko claimed he caught Doyle working on a frame, to make him—that's Belasko—look like he was ratting to the Feds."

"And you believed him."

"Doyle was dead by then," Stone said. "They had a history, all right? Doyle had been on his case since day one at the compound. Belasko had punched him out, and Doyle nursed a grudge. Open and shut."

"Now it's back open," Blankenship suggested.

"Maybe. Hell, for all I know, the two of them were in some kind of deal together, and they had a falling-out. Doyle's not important. Never was. I still don't know who he—or they—could possibly be working for. The Feds don't play like that, no warrants, shoot on sight."

"Who, then?" Blankenship asked.

Stone shrugged. "The point is, I'll know this Belasko when I see him."

"Well, you missed your chance last night. Too bad. I could of used another gun. You can describe him, though, I guess."

"Over six feet," Stone said, "around two hundred pounds. Dark hair, blue eyes, olive complexion. Some might say he looks Italian. Anyway, he's one cool customer. I never saw him smile."

"And nothing we can trust on background."

"Trust this—whatever the computers say, no matter how they lie, this guy's had tons of training. I mean, right across the board. He could be a Navy SEAL or Green Beret—hell, fucking Delta Force for all I know. The point is that he knows his shit, all right?"

Where Blankenship sat, it sounded like a sorry two-time loser trying to explain his failures, making lame excuses, but he had to grant that this guy—if it *was* one guy—had done some righteous ass-kicking the previous night. At least two dozen men were dead, with another handful unaccounted for. God help them if it turned out they had run away, then came straggling back.

"I'll put the word out through the ASA," he said, and drained his coffee in a futile effort to expunge the sour taste of failure from his mouth. "Meantime, you ought to think about some other place to hide, if you know what I'm saying. Florida gets hot enough this time of year without the extra heat you're packing."

"I'll think about it," Stone replied. His eyes were shifty, snake's eyes, as he flagged the waitress for their check. "This one's on me," he said.

Damn right, it was, Blankenship thought. It was all on him.

BRIGHT SUNSHINE STUNG Stone's eyes, until he slipped on his mirrored aviator glasses. Blankenship had left ahead of him, presumably to make some calls before he went back to the Glades, alert his fellow rednecks in the ASA to watch out for a gunman, name unknown, whose physical description had to fit twenty-five or thirty thousand men along the coast. His height aside, "Belasko" could as easily have passed for Cuban as Italian, which would make it several million suspects in Miami and environs.

Stone wouldn't hold his breath until the ASA came up with something off the streets. What kind of secret army were they, after all? A bunch of redneck, pinhead losers who ascribed their lifelong failures to the blacks, Jews, Asians, Haitians—anyone, in fact, except themselves. They couldn't face the mirror, so they shaved their heads or put some hoods on, held their meetings in the dead of night and traded lies about their prowess, all the shit they planned to do when racial holy war came down. They were pathetic.

Stone viewed them with the same disdain he normally reserved for inner-city street gangs. They were useful, though—up to a point.

It was a shame that Belasko and whoever was behind him had located Stone so quickly after Baja. He assumed that someone had been squeezed and spilled his guts, since tracking him without a lead should otherwise have demanded psychic powers. And he didn't believe that Belasko was clairvoyant. That would be too much.

Now Blankenship was asking him to leave, "suggesting" it for his own good. It had been much the same in Baja, but Stone had been ready for a change of scene before the word came down. He wasn't ready yet, in Florida. In fact, he still had work to do, more cash to earn.

No one inside the Paul Revere Militia or the ASA knew he was working for Afif Rahman, a front man for Hezbollah guerrillas, who had a bottomless reserve of petrodollars at their fingertips. Stone wondered if Belasko knew, or guessed as much, but he gained nothing from such idle speculation and he didn't like to waste his time. Instead, he should be thinking through his next six moves, anticipating opposition, plotting countermeasures to defend himself.

His mission for Rahman was vague enough to grant him several options. Hezbollah was paying Stone to foment acts of terrorism in the States that would be traceable to various domestic malcontents. The way it worked, his sponsors got a double payback on their cash investment. First, Americans were murdered, maimed, held up—whatever—in a string of crimes that made the news from coast to coast. And second, once the perpetrators were identified as American, not an Arab or outsider in the bunch, millions who were untouched by the attacks themselves would come to doubt their nation and its government, would question the policies applied to crush domestic terrorism in the form of new, restrictive state and federal legislation. All without the men behind the plan being required to squeeze a trigger or expose themselves to risk of any kind.

Stone didn't mind his role as front man for a group of strangers, foreigners who wished his native country harm. It was a mercenary's lot to serve diverse and sometimes loathsome sponsors, if the pay was right. Some mercs he knew would draw the line at working for a Communist, a black, whomever, but such fine distinctions didn't trouble him. He wanted to be rich, retire to live in style before he was too old to enjoy it. And if he survived the next few days, he would have reached his goal.

Rahman demanded one more demonstration—one "great event," as he put it—to wrap up the game. It should be something that would dominate world headlines and would leave Americans in no doubt that they had been victimized by their own "patriotic" sons and brothers. The specifics had been left to Stone's discretion, and he had a few ideas on tap.

It was a shame that they had missed the 1996 Olympics in Atlanta, but his men hadn't been organized enough to mount a campaign that ambitious, and it would have been too difficult for Stone to make his getaway. Besides, it didn't take a massacre on that scale to fulfill his contract with Rahman. He didn't need another Oklahoma City bombing, either, targeting the U.S. government specifically. In fact, Stone had an altogether different plan in mind, something a little ethnic, with the Paul Revere Militia and the ASA involved. It would make Kristallnacht in Germany look like a tea party: coordinated raids on synagogues, black churches, civil-rights groups and the like across a four-state area of Dixie, capping off a string of arson fires that had already drawn attention from the FBI and ATF.

Some of his people wanted race war, so why not let them think that it was coming, that they had a chance to put the ball in play by slinking through the night and lobbing thermite canisters or homemade Molotovs into selected buildings? And if some of those buildings were occupied, so much the better. Let some blood flow to increase the outrage that even Stone agreed was owned and operated by a pack of left-wing bleeding hearts.

It was perfect, Stone decided, but he still required some time in which to pull it off. He needed to communicate with goons in Georgia, Alabama and Mississippi to coordinate the strikes. He had to smooth some ruffled feathers in the backwaters where this or that would-be führer was competing with some other half-baked redneck for supremacy over the pointy-heads and midget-minds. Once Stone convinced them that his plan would work to everyone's advantage, he would have it locked, the strike teams set to synchronize their watches and proceed.

But he would need at least another day, and maybe two or three, to pull it off. And it would only slow him if he was forced to operate from hiding, constantly in motion, worried about someone picking up his trail. The last thing that he needed at the moment was that kind of critical distraction.

Stone knew that he could do it. All he needed was the nerve, the focus and a little time, and he could raise some hell, get paid, bail out before the shit came down.

And anyone who tried to track him after that would have to make it one-on-one. It was the kind of game Stone had been playing all his life, and he was still the master.

He was still alive.

4

Bud's Guns was located on Flagler Street, a hundred yards outside the Sweetwater city limits in suburban Dade County. The owner's name was James Westmoreland, Jr., but his friends and enemies alike all called him "Bud," for reasons no one could recall. He was a member of the Ku Klux Klan, grand cyclops of the local den, and it was known—though never proved in a court of law—that Bud Westmoreland used his federal firearms-dealer's license to keep half the morbid racists in south Florida well armed. The ATF had tried to take him down on two occasions in the past four years, but they had blown each case: the first through typos on a search warrant; the second with some sloppy record keeping that destroyed the crucial chain of evidence before his trial.

So far, old Bud was riding high.

But he had never reckoned on a visit from the Executioner.

It was high noon when Bolan strolled into the gun shop, having waited in the parking lot outside for forty minutes, making sure that he would be the only patron in the store with Westmoreland. The man was leaning on a glass display case when he entered, checking out the pictures in a shooter's magazine, lips moving slowly as he read the captions. Glancing up at Bolan with his piggy eyes, the Klansman cracked a smile and straightened, the effort sending tremors through his triple chins and rolls of flab around his waist.

"How do?" he asked by way of greeting.

"Getting warm out," Bolan answered.

"That's a fact. What can I do you for?"

A glance back toward the street showed Bolan nothing but an empty, sunbaked parking lot and sidewalk. There was no one else outside the store as yet. He had to get the place nailed down before another customer walked in and ruined everything.

"I'm new in town," he said. "Somebody told me you're the man to see."

A wrinkle formed between Westmoreland's shaggy eyebrows as he frowned in concentration. "Man to see for what?" he asked.

"Supplies, contacts," Bolan said, moving closer. "Maybe some intelligence."

Bud blinked, as if the new arrival were addressing him in Japanese. Perhaps it was the concept of intelligence that dazzled him and made a portion of his brain shut down. He frowned, trying to decide what he should say.

"Mike Baker," Bolan told him, stretching out an empty hand. "Just in from Macon."

"Bud Westmoreland."

When they shook hands, Bolan kept his first three fingers stiff so that they pressed against the inside of Bud's wrist. It was the classic "secret" handshake used by Klansmen since the 1920s, and it startled the shop owner enough to make him blink once more, as he was trying to adjust his grip.

"You're with—?"

"Teutonic Empire Knights, the same as you," Bolan said. "Imperial Knighthawk."

Westmoreland seemed impressed that a security officer

from his Klan's national headquarters would turn up in person, much less ask for his help. "You said you needed something?"

"A few minutes of your time. Is there some way we could keep from being interrupted?"

"Huh? Oh, hell, yes." The man lumbered around the counter, moving toward the door and locking it from the inside. He turned the cardboard sign around so that it told prospective patrons he was Closed, Please Try Again. "That ought to do it."

"Great," Bolan said. "Now, if you've got someplace we can talk…"

"Right here. I guarantee there's no bugs in *this* place. ATF's been after me four years, come August, and they still ain't shut me down."

"I'm well aware of your successes, Brother Bud," Bolan said, watching as Westmoreland puffed out his chest, still not rivaling his stomach. "It occurs to me, though, that somebody might be spying on us from the street. You know, the Feds use lip-readers these days."

Westmoreland blinked again, assimilating that tidbit into his mental file of paranoid imaginings. "I heard that, yeah," he said. "I wasn't sure if it were true, though."

"Take my word for it. They learned it from Mossad. You know the way those people are."

"Hell, yes." He thought about the problem for another moment, then suggested, "We could stand here, with our backs turned toward the street!"

A nod from Bolan was sufficient to remind the man of the mirror he had mounted on the shop's back wall, to help him keep an eye on shoplifters.

"You wouldn't have a back room we could use by any chance?"

Westmoreland offered him another smile. "Now, that's a fine idea! Just follow me."

The back room of the gun shop was perhaps one-third the size of the main store, but it seemed claustrophobic, all the same. Westmoreland had it stacked with crates of ammunition, more guns—still in boxes, some in plastic cases that resembled shrunken luggage—and bales of what appeared to be newspaper. Bolan checked out one of the newspaper stacks and saw a title—White Man's Burden—over headlines reading Jews Control The Media and Blacks Want Our Women!

"Just the basics here," the shop owner told him, sweeping one big hand around the cluttered room. "I can't keep any of the good stuff here, of course, what with the ATF still breathing down my neck."

"I understand," Bolan said.

"So, what brings you down this way?"

Westmoreland turned to face him, was about to park his hip against the corner of a battered military-surplus desk, when suddenly his piggy eyes went wide with shock. They focused on the black Beretta 93-R Bolan had produced from underneath his coat and pointed at the Klansman's swiftly paling face.

"YOU CAN SIT DOWN and put your hands behind your back," the stranger said. Westmoreland would have bet his life the bastard's name wasn't Mike Baker.

"Sit down?" The shock of having someone he regarded as a proud Teutonic brother pull a pistol on him in his own place had robbed Westmoreland of whatever wits and cunning he possessed.

"That's where you bend your knees and plant your ass on something that will hold your weight," the stranger told him. The Beretta wobbled toward his desk chair. "Try that, for instance."

"Oh, uh, sure."

The shop owner sat in the double-wide chair and put his hands behind his back as he was told. It was an awkward posture for a man his size, but he wasn't prepared to argue with the gun. One thing he knew was weapons. He had recognized the pistol, knew that it was capable of firing 3-round automatic bursts and that its magazine held twenty rounds. You count a live one in the tube, and that made twenty-one. The guy could strafe him seven times and turn him into dog meat if he made a sudden move.

Still, it was tempting, with the Grizzly Winchester Magnum pistol right there in the unlocked top drawer of his desk, just a foot or so away. He had guns stashed all over, ready for a robbery, but "Baker" had caught him in the dead zone, with nothing within his reach.

"Baker" stepped behind him, and Westmoreland felt the handcuffs snap around one wrist. It took some straining for the other arm to be secured, and he was tempted to try something then, but while he thought about it, he ran out of time. With both wrists cuffed, his shoulders were drawn back, spine arched, his chest and stomach presented to the gunman as a perfect target.

"What kind of Fed are you?" Westmoreland asked.

"No kind at all," the tall man told him, settling on a corner of his desk, with the Beretta dangling loose in one hand, pointed at the floor. Westmoreland thought that he could rock back in his chair, try kicking it out of the stranger's hand, but what would he do next? Sit there and grapple with the cuffs until "Baker" grabbed the piece again and wasted him, that's what.

"So, what's the deal? You knew the code."

"Bud, everybody knows the code. What I need is information. Tell me what I want to know, and maybe you'll survive another day.''

"Hey," he said, "I took a oath."

"To keep the secrets of the Klan on pain of death and torture. Right, I know."

"Well, there you go."

"The question is, Bud, where do *you* go?"

"Huh? I don't—"

"Know what I mean," the stranger finished for him. "Right. Okay. Here's how it goes. I need to find some people in your outfit. Not the Klan, specifically. The ASA. You with me so far?"

Westmoreland was frowning, wishing that he *didn't* understand. Guy comes in with a fancy pistol, asking things about the ASA, it meant he knew too much already.

The stranger didn't seem to notice Westmoreland's expression, or he didn't give a damn. "You're handy," he was saying, "and we all know you've been arming units of the ASA for months. Don't bother lying now. You need to save what breath you've got."

Bud surely didn't like the sound of *that,* but he kept quiet, did as he was told. It couldn't hurt to listen, and the more he learned about this guy, it seemed the more he would improve his chances of escape.

Or maybe not.

"Now, what I plan to do," the stranger said, "is ask you certain questions. You can answer me, and make it easy on yourself, or we can do this thing the hard way.

"You know your guns," the stranger went on. It didn't sound much like a question, but Westmoreland saw no harm in answering, regardless.

"Yeah," he said, "I do."

"You know what this is, then." His captor tapped the

stubby cylinder attached to the Beretta's muzzle with the index finger of his free hand.

"Sound suppressor?"

"That's right. It's custom-made. I only have to change the baffles every seventy or eighty shots. My thinking is, the suppressor can hold out longer than you can."

"What's that mean?" The shop owner was stalling now. He knew damn well what "Baker" meant, but if he got the guy to talk instead of doing it, he had more time. If only he could think, cook up some kind of plan instead of sitting there and sweating through his clothes.

"It means I start out with your ankles, knees and hip joints," the tall man said. "You're not big on jogging, right? I didn't think so. Then we've got the elbows and the shoulders. You'll be bleeding out by then, but all your pain receptors should be functioning."

He made it sound so clinical that Westmoreland could picture it, the bullets smashing into him, ripping his joints apart and leaving him a cripple even if he didn't bleed to death or take a final round behind the ear. He didn't know how much of that he could take, and suddenly his oath of silence took a back seat to the instinct for self-preservation. He could wrestle with his conscience later, if he lived that long. Right now, he simply wanted to keep breathing.

"Okay, shoot," Westmoreland said, then caught himself. "No, wait! I mean to say, go on and ask your questions."

"First of all," his captor said, "I need a list of outfits in the ASA, for confirmation purposes."

That wasn't hard. The Feds knew most of that, anyway. "Teutonic Empire Knights, you know about. There's the Paul Revere Militia and the Death's-Head SS Action

Team. Let's see…oh, yeah. Dade County Minutemen. They don't add up to much.''

"You know the men in charge for southern Florida?''

"I guess.''

The 93-R twitched, its muzzle rising to the level of his knees. "Say what?'' the tall man asked.

"I know them, yeah. You want names? It's Amos Hardy for the Empire Knights, and Virgil Blankenship for the militia. SS Action's got a new guy, since their captain went away behind explosives charges. Darren something, I don't know. The Minutemen don't really have a leader, but there's only ten or fifteen of them, anyway, I think. Like I already said, they don't add up to much.''

"Not like the Klan and Paul Reveres,'' the stranger said.

"You got that right,'' Westmoreland answered proudly. "We been taking care of business.''

"I'll just bet you have. We've had a lot of church fires down this way. Some vandalism aimed at synagogues. Assault and battery. Some drive-bys.''

Westmoreland was smiling, but he knew he couldn't talk about that. For all he knew this guy was wired, his every comment broadcast to a tape recorder, maybe sitting in a van outside the shop.

"I wouldn't know about that stuff, but if the nig—''

An open palm caught Bud's right cheek and rocked his head, the sound of impact ringing like a pistol shot. His face was numb for just a second, then the pain and angry heat enveloped him.

"Hey, what the fuck!''

This time a backhand stunned him. He tasted something salty in his mouth and knew it had to be blood. His ears were ringing, and he had to blink hot tears of pain away before he could regain his focus on the man standing over him.

"Don't feed me that," the stranger told him, sounding icy cold. "I'm here for information, not some paranoid bullshit about the master race, all right?"

"Uh-huh."

"You know Chris Stone?"

"I met him once. Seen him around a couple other times. He don't live here."

"My information is, he's planning something special for the ASA. I'm betting you know what that is."

Westmoreland had to think about it for a moment. He had a hunch what "Baker" was getting at, but if he spilled it... If he *didn't*...

"Well?"

"He talked about some hits," Westmoreland said, deciding he would rather live than be a martyr to the cause. "I don't got any details. Something big, is what he said. I got the drift it was a bunch of places being taken down at the same time, all over, like."

"He'd have a list of targets?" the stranger asked.

"Not that I saw. You'd have to ask somebody with some rank about the rest of it."

"I guess I'll just do that."

The Executioner rapped the butt of the Beretta against Westmoreland's temple. A quick call to Brognola would have a mop-up crew in the area in a half hour. The gunshop owner would be put on ice in some isolated area until the mission was over, thereby preventing him from alerting the militia.

The Executioner would be making another foray into the swamp.

5

The sun was bright and hot when Bolan reached the Everglades, but there was shade among the cypress trees and mangroves as he worked his way into the swamp. The outboard motor on his Zodiac boat cut through the floating layer of scum that veiled the water's surface, laying down a foot-wide trail behind him. But the swamp couldn't be beaten, and the floating algae soon closed ranks again, wiped out his track as if no one had ever passed that way.

And that was fine with Bolan, since he didn't need to advertise his presence.

As on his first probe of the swamp, he killed the outboard better than a mile out from his target, taking up an oar and finishing the job by hand. Long, nearly silent strokes powered him along, and he avoided thicker stands of saw grass where he could, referring to his compass when he lost the sun behind the treetops.

Bud Westmoreland had regained consciousness when the retrieval team had arrived on the scene. Under additional questioning, he revealed the time and place of war games scheduled by the ASA, presumably including members of the several far-right groups that had combined to form the secret army. Inasmuch as Bolan had no other leads on Stone, he reckoned that it couldn't hurt to drop in on the games and raise a little hell while he was in the neighborhood, provide the weekend warriors with a taste of what *real* war was all about. And if he got a lead to his primary target in the process, why, so much the better.

He was armed much as he had been on his night raid at the Paul Revere Militia's camp, some miles away to the southeast. His lead weapon was different from the one he'd carried on his first strike in the swamp: a Heckler & Koch MP-5 SD-3 submachine gun, with a telescoping butt and factory-installed suppressor. Slung beneath his arm, the customized Beretta 93-R also had its "silencer" in place. Both guns wore condoms on their muzzles, held in place by rubber bands, to keep the barrels dry while he was closing with his targets once he left the Zodiac behind.

Bolan's plan was relatively simple: find the troops engaged in their maneuvers, infiltrate their ranks and raise whatever hell he could. It didn't sound that difficult in theory, but the men he hunted weren't his only problem in the Glades, where Mother Nature could be every bit as deadly as a firing squad equipped with M-16s. One false step anywhere along the way, and he was history. The swamp would gladly swallow him alive, and he would simply cease to be.

He felt mosquitoes nipping at his flesh but resisted the impulse to slap them, since the sound might carry for a quarter-mile or more across the water. He could live with the discomfort, and the tiny loss of blood was nothing in comparison to what he faced if he allowed the enemy to know that he was coming.

Still a half mile from the designated target zone, he piloted the Zodiac beneath an arch of giant mangrove roots and tied it off. Cattails and saw grass served to further camouflage the small inflatable craft. He eased into the water, waiting for his boots to find some purchase in the muck, testing it to see how deeply he would sink when he released his grip. The water reached his hips, but he couldn't rely on any constant depth, aware that it could change with every yard he traveled. If both feet got stuck, he would be forced to float, allow the water's buoyancy to take his weight, while he laboriously, gently worked each boot free of the sucking mud and silt.

The trick was to not get stuck, though, if he could help it. The idea of normal movement in the Glades, for men on foot, was ludicrous, but Bolan's adversaries would be dealing with the same handicaps. Unless they brought the airboats in, their sole advantage would be numbers, and he meant to shave those odds with stealth.

In Southeast Asia, in another life, such work had been his specialty. Bolan had led a group called Pen Team Able—"Pen" for *Pen*etration, as in long-range hunting in the enemy's backyard. In those days, he had done much of his hunting with a sniper's rifle, but the basic concept was the same. He simply needed to be closer now to make his kills.

No sweat.

The swamp was his accomplice, though it couldn't be mistaken for an ally. Nature took no sides, determined only that the fittest would survive to feed and breed. Man tipped the balance, with his clothing, tools and weapons, but no matter how he stacked the deck, he never really changed the nature of the game.

Bolan had come to play, and he was betting everything he had. When they were dealt, his cards might come up winners, or they might turn out to be a dead man's hand. Whichever way it went, the Executioner knew only one way to proceed. He bet the limit every time, and always called the opposition's bluff. This day would be no different, however it turned out.

When he was steady on his feet—as steady as the

swamp allowed, at any rate—the Executioner retrieved his submachine gun from the Zodiac and double-checked his other gear. A moment later, he was moving through the hip-deep water, through the shallows, hunting for his prey.

CHAD TUCKER DIDN'T CARE for swamp maneuvers, but he knew a soldier had to be prepared for anything, around the clock. It was a frigging inconvenience giving up his weekend to go sloshing through the Glades, but he had known the job would have a downside when he took it. Things were getting worse each day in the United States, with crime and the economy, race mixing, godless humanism spreading poison in the schools, all kinds of filth on television every time he turned it on.

Okay, so maybe that part didn't bother him so much, but all the rest of it was bullshit, and it had to stop.

Chad Tucker held the rank of titan in the Ku Klux Klan, Teutonic Empire Knights. In theory, that made him responsible for all the Klansmen in a "dominion"—Ku Kluxese for a congressional district—but they didn't have sufficient members yet to organize along those lines, so Tucker had been given all Dade County to supervise and keep the boys in line. He kept an eye on the recruiters, took his bit of what they earned and did his best to keep the major misfits in the group from going off half-cocked and doing something that would bring the heat down on them all.

Those times were changing, though. Since the Teutonic Empire Knights had signed on with the ASA, some thirteen months earlier, there had been talk of great things in the works, and night riding had escalated. It was more like in the old days that his daddy talked about sometimes when he was drinking: going out at night to whip black ass or plant a bomb, some shit like that. And bigger things were coming down the road.

Preparedness was everything, Tucker realized. The blacks and Jews were organized, with the police behind them, and the white man had to do the same. Get ready for the day of judgment, hone his skills, stockpile his hardware. He who hesitated was lost, and no mistake.

A cottonmouth went wriggling past him, maybe three feet to his left, and Tucker let it go. The AR-15 he was carrying had twenty blank rounds in its magazine, and while the Browning semiauto pistol in his shoulder rig was packing live ones, he didn't need the noise right now. They had a job to do, despite the heat and snakes, the muck, mosquitoes and the misery of slogging through the Glades.

Somebody cursed behind him, and he turned to reprimand the loose-lipped Klansman. Automatically, before he spoke, Tucker counted heads, the way he always did when they were out on war games, making sure nobody wandered off, got lost or went to find himself a six-pack. There were ten, eleven, twelve, thirteen…

"Where's Jackson?" he demanded, shifting to his left and scanning back along the line.

"He's right back—" Eddie Wix, the next-to-last in line when they set out, had turned around to look, and he was gaping at the empty space behind him, where Doug Jackson should have been. "Hey, where is he?"

"All right, now, keep it down!" Tucker snapped, moving back along the line. "We still got people hunting us, in case you disremember."

"Yeah, but—"

"Yeah-but nothing!" He was glaring hard at Wix now. "Get your ass back there and find him, double-quick! We haven't got all day."

"Why me?"

"Because he was next in line to you," Tucker said, "and the two of you are teamed up for this exercise. Because I fucking said so, if you need a better reason."

"Yeah, okay. I'm going."

"'Yeah, I'm going, *sir*,'" Tucker corrected him, and stood there, staring hard at Wix until he got the point.

"I'm going, *sir*."

"So, move. You got five minutes, or we leave without the both of you."

Wix didn't need five minutes, as it turned out. He was back in under two, high stepping through the muck and splashing up a storm, trailing the buttstock of his weapon in the water as he ran, red-faced and panting, nearly falling as he caught up to the team again. It took another moment for the obviously frightened man to catch his breath, before he could communicate in anything approximating English.

"Juh-Juh-Jackson! Found him! He...he's dead!"

"Say what?" Tucker couldn't believe his ears. "What do you mean, he's dead?"

"Back there," Wix told him, waving vaguely toward the green hell of the Glades behind him. "Stuck up in some roots, like. Swear to God, he's dead."

"What happened?"

"How the hell should I know, *sir?*"

"All right, goddammit. Show me!"

"Huh?"

"You heard me, Wix. If Jackson's dead, I need to see him for myself and try to figure out what happened."

"Jesus Christ."

"Pray on your own time, boy. We got a job to do."

They backtracked fifty yards or so. Jackson was hung up in mangrove roots, almost as if he was posed there for the rest of them to find, and he was dead. No doubt about it.

Tucker didn't know what to expect, but he moved closer to examine the dead Klansman. Snakebite could be fatal in the Glades, he knew, but not that fast, and Jackson would have started raising hell if he was bitten. Anyway, a snakebite wouldn't make him bleed that way, the crimson soaking through his camouflage fatigue shirt, turning it all rust brown.

Up close, the source of all that blood was readily apparent. Jackson's throat was cut almost from ear to ear—the windpipe, jugular, carotid arteries, the whole nine yards. Tucker backed off from the body, mouthing curses as the mud sucked at his boots.

"Somebody killed him," Tucker told his troops.

"Huh?"

"What do you mean, *somebody* killed him?" Tommy Decker asked.

"What I said. Somebody took a knife and cut his throat down to the backbone. Is that plain enough?"

"I never heard a thing, for Christ's sake," Wix stated. "Jesus, he was right behind me, all the time."

"Shut up and let me think!" the titan ordered. "And for God's sake, don't start yammering. We're in a whole new ball game now."

THE FIRST ONE HAD BEEN easy, lagging back and breaking discipline to light a cigarette and smoke it on the sly. It cost him. Bolan glided up behind the careless Klansman like a shadow. One hand was clamped across his mouth to wrench his head back, while his other brought around the Ka-bar fighting knife to do its work. The man grappled with the Executioner for a moment, trying hopelessly to catch the fleeting spark of life before it guttered out, and then he was deadweight in Bolan's arms. A few more seconds to prepare his body, prop it up just so, and he was done.

He waited, watching as the first Klansman came back to look for his companion, spotted him and made a hasty check to verify that life had fled. The searcher took off splashing then, and brought a dozen others with him when he came back moments later. Bolan recognized them, had been trailing them for better than a quarter hour when he saw the chance to make his kill, and he was ready for them now. The range was twenty yards. He couldn't miss.

His submachine gun fired 800 rounds per minute on full-auto, meaning it could eat the contents of a 30-round box magazine in 2.25 seconds, but the situation called for more precise delivery of fire, so he had set the H&K for 3-round bursts. No problem. Twenty yards was next to point-blank range for that piece in those hands.

He chose a target, picking out the tallest of the thirteen Klansmen, six foot two or three, red-faced beneath his boonie hat, mouth almost hidden by a scraggly beard and mustache. He held the H&K's sights steady on his target's chest, butt braced against his shoulder as he gently drew the trigger back.

Three parabellum shockers ripped into the Klansman's rib cage, crimson jets exploding from the holes that had opened in his chest. He toppled backward with a splash, dead when he fell, and his companions turned to gape at him.

"Hey, what—?"

"Jesus, Hank, you gotta watch out where you—"

"Shit! Incoming! Scatter!"

Loaded with subsonic rounds, the MP-5 SD-3 submachine gun was as silent as technology could make it. There was still a muffled popping sound for every shot, no louder than a pellet gun using compressed-air cartridges, and Bolan heard the *click-clack* of the flying bolt as each spent casing was ejected. Twenty yards away, with everybody speaking at once and splashing through the water, searching desperately for cover, it would be inaudible.

Which didn't mean, however, that the Klansmen couldn't spot him. They had missed their chance with Hank, too startled by his death to backtrack in the direction where the fatal shots had come from, but each time he pulled the trigger, Bolan would be giving them another chance.

Too bad.

He squeezed off two more bursts, one target pitching forward, slammed between the shoulder blades, while to his left, another staggered, wounded but still mobile, thrashing toward a nearby cypress tree for cover. Bolan left him to it, tracking other Klansmen, wondering how many he could tag before one of them spotted him.

Some of his enemies were firing back instinctively, but from the sound of it he knew that they were shooting blanks. It was a waste of time, but they apparently were hoping that the random fire would keep his head down, spoil his aim, whatever. Bolan knew that some of them would doubtless have a magazine or two of live rounds stashed away to help discourage alligators and the like. Kluxers loved guns, and they were never far removed from firepower, but at the moment, he still held the upper hand.

Running was difficult in hip-deep water, all the more so when combat boots were ankle or calf deep in clinging muck. Bolan was thankful now for the topography he had been cursing earlier, when it had slowed him and forced him to take extra care with splashing noises that could easily betray him. Standing with his forward elbow braced atop a slimy mangrove root, he framed another fleeing target in his sights and sent three parabellum rounds to take the runner down. The dying man cried out, a wordless bleat of pain and panic, as he plunged headfirst into the brackish water.

Suddenly a couple of the Klansmen were charging straight at Bolan, lurching steps propelling them along. They didn't seem to see him, but were making for the mangrove he had chosen as his cover, seemingly oblivious to death before them, even as he fired and took their comrades down.

Okay. A master sniper never looked a gift horse in the mouth. Instead of ducking back, perhaps abandoning his shelter, Bolan met them with a double burst that left him only nine rounds in his weapon's magazine. Three manglers left their bloody tracks across one Klansman's upper torso, spinning him so that he landed in the water on his back, arms flailing as he fell. The other took his in the face and throat, stone dead on impact, taking one more awkward stride before his muscles got the message from a ruptured brain and he went down.

"I see him! Shit!"

One of the Kluxers had a semiauto pistol in his hand—make that both hands, the classic combat stance—and when he fired at Bolan, there was no mistaking the report of live rounds going off, the snap of bullets passing overhead. Immediately the Executioner shifted slightly to his right and made target acquisition, squeezing off one burst, another and a third.

The gunner staggered, wasting two rounds on the sky above him as he toppled, bellowing in pain, conscious of the fact that he had failed his unit and himself. If anybody else had registered his words and followed the direction of his shots, none was prepared to act upon that knowledge of the adversary's whereabouts. Each was consumed with finding cover for himself before it was too late.

The Executioner reloaded, ditched his empty magazine and went back to the killing game. He might not drop them all, but he could try, and when his work was done with this squad, there were others waiting for him, even if they didn't know it yet.

And Bolan didn't plan to keep them waiting long.

THE SOUNDS OF GUNFIRE startled Darren Lowery, brought him to a halt with one hand raised, a silent signal to his men. Behind him, fifteen members of the Death's-Head SS Action Team stopped on a dime, their discipline a credit to their leaders. Each man stood, listening and waiting, hard eyes studying the swampland that surrounded Lowery and his rifle squad.

They had been slogging through the Glades since shortly after sunrise, and there was still no contact with the "enemy," consisting of selected Klansmen and militia members who wore red armbands, in contrast to the blue displayed by Lowery's team and the Dade County Minutemen. A long, hot, filthy morning lay behind them, and it wasn't getting any cooler in the swamp the closer it moved on toward noon. Lowery was frustrated, knew that his troops were getting antsy, but a war game wasn't simply trading blank rounds with your opposition. It incorporated strategy, evasion and pursuit, survival in a simulated combat zone.

So far, they had sustained no casualties, real or imaginary, and the game was getting old. Now this. When Lowery tried to work out the direction that the sounds were coming from, he felt a moment of confusion, cursing the terrain that all looked pretty much the same, no matter where you went around the Glades. Some parts of it had more large trees, like here, but there was always saw grass, reeds that gave the leeches access to your clothes and flesh. The team had several compasses, together with a hand-drawn, laminated map of the selected hunting ground, but it was only so much help when you were ass deep in the swamp, with alligators all around.

Who would be firing? Lowery asked himself, and knew the answer: anybody. They had chosen sides by lot, with the Teutonic Empire Knights dividing up because they were more numerous, the Paul Revere Militia coming up with fewer men than promised after some kind of a problem at their camp, not far away from where the Death's-Head SS Action Team was standing now. Armbands had been distributed, and six teams had been dropped at different points on the perimeter of the engagement area, to find their way—and find their prey—as best they could.

Now, from the sound of it, the battle had been joined. The racket seemed to come from straight ahead, although the swamp could be deceptive, with its echoes and occasional disorienting silence. Lowery made it north-northwest of their position, but he couldn't calculate the distance well enough to risk a guess. Sounds had been known to carry for miles in the swamp, while others were diverted, muffled by the undergrowth and swallowed up before they reached your ears.

"This way," he told his pointman, indicating the direction with a nod. They hadn't traveled far before the sounds of combat died away, replaced in time by birdcalls and the sounds of buzzing insects.

So the engagement had been fast and furious, a brief encounter. Since both sides had left off firing, Lowery had to guess that one group was annihilated by the other. Maybe someone had prepared an ambush, caught a team with the wrong-colored armbands passing by, oblivious to danger on their flanks. That kind of negligence could get you killed, no less in downtown Hollywood, Coral Gables or Miami Beach, as in the Everglades.

Lowery was proud of his command. The Death's-Head SS Action Team was relatively young, as neo-Nazi cadres went, but they had shaped up well in two years' time. Lowery insisted that his soldiers translate their beliefs to action, keep themselves in shape and practice with their weapons at least once a week. He hadn't taken to the idea of a merger with the ASA at first, but he had been persuaded by the numbers and the opportunity to fight for what his men believed in, rather than debating it to death and spending all their time composing endless diatribes against the Jews. What was the point in heading up an action team unless you saw some action now and then?

The day was coming when his enemies would weep and grovel at his feet, but that would only happen after they were taught a lesson of humility, reminded that it was not safe to leave their place. And when the party had control...

He snapped back from his reverie as something wet and slimy dropped onto his nape. Blunt fingers found the leech before it could attach itself, and Lowery tossed it from him with an easy backhand. Plop, and it was gone.

Black bastards, sucking a man's blood before they crept away somewhere to breed in filth and start the cycle all over again. If he could snap his fingers and eliminate them all, Lowery would do exactly that.

And they would have a lot of company.

Ahead of him, some thirty yards or so, the pointman gave a muffled cry and went down on his face. Lowery suppressed an impulse to call out and ask him what was wrong, imagining that he had simply lost his footing in the muck, expecting him to rise again, continue on.

But he wasn't getting up.

Lowery stopped dead and clutched the AK-47 to his chest as if it could protect him with its load of blanks. The pointman wasn't moving, facedown in the scummy water, and from where he stood, Lowery could see no bubbles rising near his head.

Now what?

But he had a sneaking hunch, and Lowery didn't like it one bit, a sense of something just about to hit the fan. His hands were trembling as he yanked the AK's magazine, replaced it in a belt pouch and found another—this one with a little dab of green paint on the side, and fed it into the receiver.

"Live rounds," he commanded. "Pass it on."

BOLAN COULDN'T BE SURE which unit of the ASA he had encountered, but it made no difference from a practical standpoint. The teams were distinguished by colored armbands, for purposes of identification during the war games, but they were all the same in Bolan's eyes. One group might hate the Jews more than they hated blacks, for instance, but the driving force behind the coalition as a whole was the intent to launch a "holy war" of sorts against the government of the United States. Subversive to a man, the several different contingents of the ASA were all in line for visits from the Executioner.

Bolan had left the first squad in disarray, with three or four survivors wounded, thrashing aimlessly amid the saw grass, trying desperately to hide. The latest targets wore blue armbands, rather than the crimson of the first team, and they showed a bit more discipline in their formation as they plodded through the swamp.

He dropped the pointman with a single shot from his Beretta and was holstering the pistol, reaching for the SMG he carried slung across one shoulder, even as the body toppled over with a splash. The dead man's companions stopped short in their tracks, the leader issuing an order Bolan couldn't hear, but its effect was obvious. As one, the weekend warriors pulled the magazines out of their weapons and began to replace them with others drawn from bandoliers or ammo pouches on their belts.

And that could only mean one thing.

He sighted on the man who seemed to be the leader of the team, a stocky man who wore a toothbrush mustache to enhance the Hitler likeness. Bolan gave him three rounds in the chest and watched him sink while the remainder of his team was trying to make sense of what had happened to the pointman.

They were way too late. The parabellum bullets from his submachine gun whispered among them, raising little water spouts when Bolan missed his mark or one of them ripped through a body and kept going. Several of the would-be storm troopers were firing aimlessly into the murky swamp, using live rounds from the sound of it, but none came close to Bolan as he picked and chose his targets, emptying one magazine, replacing it, continuing the slaughter.

Ninety seconds after it had started, there was nothing moving in his field of fire. He couldn't tell if all of them were dead, nor did he care. A badly wounded soldier, stranded in the Everglades, would need a miracle to last the afternoon.

But there were other targets waiting for him not so far away.

The Executioner moved out to find them, hardly glancing at his map and compass, following his nose for death.

6

His friends could bitch and moan all that they wanted to, but Barney Echols liked these little outings in the Everglades. He didn't mind the muck or the mosquitoes, watching out for water moccasins and dodging alligators, leeches, being soaked from the waist down most of the time. Where others saw a hardship, Echols saw a challenge he could master with determination and a strength of will.

It wasn't like his daily life at all, the smirking insults he endured at his job from better-educated co-workers, the women who rejected him because of his big ears and crooked teeth, the fifteen-year-old car he had been driving—and repairing—for what seemed like half his life. Out here, he knew what he was doing, and the others sensed that in him, asking Echols for advice about which plants were safe to eat, which snakes were dangerous, the best way to maintain a campsite in the all-pervasive damp and rot. At times like this, he knew that joining the Dade County Minutemen had been the smartest move he ever made.

Or that's what he thought before they walked into a firestorm and his friends began to drop like flies.

Someone was shooting live rounds at them, using some kind of a silencer. Echols had figured that out for himself, when Jack Davis took one in the face, no more than ten or fifteen feet in front of him, and his brains flew out a fist-sized exit wound behind one ear. It didn't take a ton of bricks to fall on Echols and alert him to the fact that they were in a pickle. He had dived for cover instantly, wormed underneath some mangrove roots, and he was still there, with the water up around his armpits, trying not to let his Mini-14 rifle take a soaking in the process.

As it turned out, knowing what the danger was and taking steps to counteract it were two very different things. The more he tried to come up with some kind of strategy, the more it seemed to him that his brain was frozen, the machinery jammed so tight you couldn't squeak a notion through with twenty pounds of Vaseline. He just kept thinking about escaping, but little things like where he ought to go and how he would survive the run eluded him.

Like everybody in his unit, Echols carried live rounds in addition to the blanks they used for war games, and he had already switched his magazines, lips moving as he prayed the 5.56 mm rounds weren't ruined by their soaking in the marsh. He reckoned they should be all right, at least for now, but he didn't have a target anyway, so what damn difference did it make?

A body floated facedown ten or fifteen feet away from where Echols hid among the mangrove roots. Stu Turner had been shot down from behind while he was running, seeking somewhere safe to hide. Echols had seen him die, worked out the sniper's rough position from the way the first round plunked into the water just behind Stu, and the others ripped into his back, one bursting from his abdomen below the breast bone, squirting blood. Echols couldn't have pointed to the gunman just from that, but he knew that the man—or *men,* since there could be more than one—was somewhere on the other side of the tree, or west, and close enough to nail a moving target just as easy as you please.

When it first started, Echols had assumed that someone on the red team had to have loaded live rounds by mistake, and they would realize it in a moment, when they saw the blood and bodies floating in the swamp. But he or they kept shooting, and it came to him that the sniper couldn't be part of the exercise, since no one in the ASA had brought a silencer along on the maneuvers.

Had they? Why would anybody on the team start shooting his white Christian brothers in the middle of the Glades?

When Echols couldn't answer that, he started running down a mental list of others who would love to take some potshots at the ASA. He thought of the Black Liberation Unit and the Sword of Judah, one cranked up on hate for whitey, while the other threatened anyone who didn't worship Israel as a holy paradise on earth. There was an Arab group in Boca he had heard about, supposed to be Iranians, allegedly receiving money from Khaddafi on the sly. You had your Cubans everywhere, demanding signs and ballots printed up in Spanish at the taxpayers' expense, while they took welfare from the state. So what if most of them were anti-Castro? You could look at them and tell they had no love for gringos or the country that had sheltered them when they were on the run from Communist oppression in their native land.

Too many possibilities, and thinking hard made Echols's head ache. It was time for him to do something, at least to make a run for it instead of hiding and watching while the men around him died.

Reluctantly he wriggled out from underneath the mangrove roots, still kept the tree between himself and where he thought the sniper was hiding, more or less. A break to right or left would put him in the clear, an easy target, but if he ran straight out from the mangrove tree, almost due east, he might just have a chance. If he could make a hundred yards, there were more trees for cover, saw grass that could hide him even as it slashed his face and hands.

He started to slog through the brackish water, the deep muck dragging on his feet with every step. Still, he was making progress, getting somewhere. Just a few more moments, and—

A giant fist struck Barney Echols square between the shoulder blades, and he went down. His last thought, as the water closed above his head, was that death didn't hurt the way he had expected. Hell, this wasn't bad at all.

In fact, he didn't feel a damned thing.

THE RUNNER WENT DOWN with a solid splash, and Bolan swept his SMG across the killing zone in search of other targets. They were thinning, a few survivors hiding out, and it would be more trouble than he needed going after them. Complete annihilation wasn't vital to his plan; in fact, it wouldn't hurt if there were some survivors who could spread the word around, perhaps unnerve the enemies who missed this little hoedown in the Everglades.

The third team he had ambushed wore blue armbands, and most of them were packing hardware that the media would have called assault weapons. In fact, Bolan saw when they began returning fire, fully half of the rifles were civilian semiautomatic models, but with live rounds in their magazines, they packed a killing punch.

Two gunners armed with Colt AR-15s had taken cover in the shadow of a giant cypress, hung with trailing Spanish moss. Bolan wasn't sure whether they had spotted him, but they kept popping out to fire, one man on each side of the tree, and they were sending bullets in his general direction, whether through dumb luck or by design. The rounds weren't coming close enough to worry him, but Bolan thought he might as well dispose of them before he let the stragglers off the hook and went in search of other prey.

He started to circle to his left, using the saw grass as a screen, taking the cuts he couldn't manage to avoid. His passage made the tall grass sway, but if his adversaries noticed it, they gave no sign, still firing back in the direction he had come from, indicating that they didn't have him spotted, after all.

Tough luck.

Once he was on the hunt, the Executioner preferred to follow through. When he had covered thirty yards or so, he faced the cypress—visible above the sharp-edged stand of saw grass—and unclipped a frag grenade. He dropped its safety pin into the water, edging closer to his prey until he had a clear view of the tree down to the waterline. He couldn't hope to kill them both with the grenade—indeed, he couldn't guarantee that either one of them would stop a single bit of shrapnel—but the move was worth a try.

He made the pitch, a looping overhand toss, and saw a splash as the grenade came down behind the cypress tree. A heartbeat later it exploded underwater, sending up a mucky green geyser that showered upon his enemies.

One of the shooters staggered into view, his rifle trailing in the water, while his free hand clawed the peat and algae from his eyes. Still blind, he took a 3-round burst from Bolan's SMG and went down to his knees, nothing but eyebrows, forehead and a shock of sandy hair still visible above the water's surface, even that lost as he fell over onto his side.

The second gunner broke away to Bolan's right. He

came out firing from the hip, but he had no idea where his enemy was situated, laying down a screen of fire that might have helped him in another situation but was worse than useless here. The H&K spit out another burst of triplets, and the soldier seemed to trip on something underwater, screaming as he fell to rise no more. Instead of turning red with blood, the water that surrounded him went darker brown.

How many left from this team? Bolan estimated four or five of the original fourteen, and guessed that one or two of those were wounded. He could stay and seek them out, or he could go in search of other targets, sharing his attention with as many members of the ASA as possible while there was time.

He chose diversity, reloading as he backed away through saw grass six feet tall. Westmoreland had suggested that between one hundred and 150 weekend soldiers would be joining in the Everglades maneuvers, and Bolan had already dealt with nearly one-third of the higher number.

Bolan kept on moving, heading off to the northeast. Mosquitoes rose in clouds around him, and he made no effort to avoid them as he started looking for another rifle team to waste.

This morning, there was blood enough to go around.

BOB SACKETT STILL couldn't believe that he was back here in the Everglades again. Gung ho or not, he could have used a break, but Blankenship had ordered him to lead the Paul Revere contingent in the scheduled ASA war games. They were attempting to conceal the raid against their base—involving the authorities would raise too many questions that were better left unanswered, after all—and if they didn't show for the maneuvers, tongues would start to wag. Inevitably someone would question their commitment to the cause, and Blankenship wouldn't let that happen while he still had soldiers fit to take to the field and show their stuff.

Sackett had thirteen gunners on his team, an equal number marching from the far side of the target zone. They all wore red armbands, at his insistence, so that none of them would have to fire on comrades when a firefight started. Of course, the "enemies" were all his comrades, too, at least in theory, but it didn't feel the same. Sackett regarded his troops as unique, a cut above the rest, despite the beating they had taken only two nights earlier. The intervening day had calmed him a bit, but not entirely. There was still a sense of being shadowed, watched, as they proceeded through the stinking swamp to reach their goal.

Sackett was miserable, sweating buckets, blinking perspiration from his eyes and trying not to let his AR-15 duck below the surface of the water. Every now and then he faltered, feeling something brush against his legs and wondering what it could be—a snake, an eel, some other kind of fish. He had been hearing stories lately of piranhas in the Glades, supposedly illegal pets that had been dumped to save their owners from a hefty fine, but he reckoned that was bullshit. There were ample dangers in the swamp, without importing little monsters from the Amazon to make it worse.

How long had they been marching through the waist-deep water? It felt like days, but Sackett's watch told him it had been five hours and thirty-seven minutes. They would break for lunch soon, and he could already hear the complaining when, inevitably, one or two of his commandos found that they had failed to double-check the seal on plastic bags they carried in their fanny packs. It never failed.

Sackett was looking for a likely place to stop and rest, a hummock that would let them crawl out of the water for a while, when suddenly he heard the fierce, insectile whine of bullets zipping through the humid air. At first he thought it had to be hornets, since the last outburst of firing—blanks, at that—had been some twenty minutes earlier, away to the southwest of his position, but the fantasy evaporated when a soldier three men back in line cried out and fell over.

Another member of the rifle team was reaching for his fallen comrade, asking what the hell was wrong with him, when Sackett saw his face and throat explode. One moment, he was laughing at his comrade's clumsiness, and then his lower face dissolved into a crimson mist, and he went over backward, glassy eyed, probably dead before he hit the water.

"Scatter!" Sackett bellowed to his troops. "Heads down! We're under fire!"

There were still no reports of gunfire, and he knew what that meant when you coupled it with live rounds ripping through his men. The nightmare was repeating, dammit, and he felt his scrotum shrivel at the prospect of another dance with death there in the Glades.

The first thing he required was cover, and he found it in the saw grass, hunching over like a coolie picking rice, so that the four- and five-foot blades would hide him from his enemies. The grass wouldn't stop bullets, though, and Sackett was already moving toward the nearest stand of cypress trees, remembering the night he had gone hunting for a faceless adversary in the swamp and lost his team. This time, if he was fortunate, the trees might save his ass instead of sheltering his enemy.

More bullets whispered through the saw grass, missing him by inches. Sackett's men were firing now, at least a couple of them using blanks, while others had been smart enough to slip in magazines of live rounds that they carried on maneuvers as insurance against bears and alligators. Sackett wondered whether any of them knew what they were shooting at. He hoped they found a target, willed them to aim true and nail the bastards who were forcing him to run and hide a second time.

There was only so much running that a man could do before he lost faith in himself, his manhood, and began to wonder whether he was yellow after all. Sackett hadn't reached that point as yet, but he was gaining on it. There he was, supposed to be a leader and an example to his men when they were under fire, but all he could think about was looking out for number one.

To hell with it! The war he had signed on to fight bore no resemblance to the battle they were fighting now. Sackett had been expecting midnight raids and drive-bys, possibly some bombings, but in those scenarios, *his* people did the raiding and the bombing, while their enemies stood back and made arrangements for the funerals. How could it be that after all their paramilitary training, after all the speeches they had listened to, the Paul Reveres were on the verge of getting whipped again?

He lost his footing once, twice, feeling saw grass slash his cheeks and scalp, fresh wounds among the others that had just begun to heal. He didn't even want to think about what he would look like when this day was over, since he didn't know if he would be alive. That kind of thinking could distract a man at crucial moments, turn his thoughts of sudden death into a self-fulfilling prophecy. He needed every ounce of concentration he could muster just to keep himself alive.

It crossed his mind that something might have happened to the other teams, as well. They had been hearing gunfire off and on all morning—skirmishes, he told himself, until the sound of an explosion echoed through the swamp from somewhere to the west of their position. That had puzzled him and started some of Sackett's people asking questions, since nobody was supposed to bring grenades along on war games. He had silenced them at last, told them that they would find out what had happened when their work was finished. In the meantime, they had better keep their mouths shut and their eyes wide-open if they didn't want the Teutonic Empire Knights or some of Darren's goose steppers to take them by surprise.

One of his men was screaming now, as if in pain, and there was nothing Sackett could do about it. Sergeant's stripes or no, he couldn't deal with enemies who were invisible, with silenced weapons. Hell, he couldn't even *find* the bastards, much less take them out all by himself.

It occurred to Sackett that he hadn't swapped his magazine of blanks for live rounds, and he did so in a hurry, almost dropping the replacement mag before he got it right. At last, now he would have a fair chance to defend himself.

BOLAN WAS TIRING of the game and running short of ammunition, pausing to select another target as surviving members of the fourth team he had ambushed ran and splashed in search of cover, shouting questions, curses, firing blindly into the swamp. It was a little glimpse of hell on earth, and not the first that he had seen by any means.

He hadn't planned to work his way through every team, one hundred or so men in all. It would have taken him all day, if he could manage it alone, and he was already fatigued from slogging through the swamp since shortly after dawn. His infiltration and disruption of the war game was a gesture more than anything, to show his enemies that there was no safe haven, no place they could hide or carry out their business without facing retribution from the Executioner. Still, there was only so much he could do in one place at one time.

He primed a frag grenade, lined up his mark and let it fly. Six seconds later, the explosion raised a water spout and thrust a broken body skyward. For a moment, there was silence in the swamp, then a few of Bolan's adversaries started to fire back again, trying to slaughter shadows, all their sound and fury wasted.

Bolan went to join them, moving closer, tracking on the sounds of guns and voices, ducking underneath the rounds that clipped saw grass and cattails, gouged the bark from trees.

He missed the soldier hiding in the shadow of a looming cypress bole until they were within six feet of each other. Why the cringing soldier didn't simply shoot him, Bolan didn't understand, but something made the guy rush out from cover, bellowing an incoherent war cry, looking for some kind of hand-to-hand action. The Executioner was there to meet him, swinging up the barrel of his submachine gun, smashing it into the soldier's face with force enough to stagger him. Blood streamed from his lips and nose as he went over backward, splashing into the swamp water.

The guy was spitting blood as he thrashed amid the saw grass, taking new wounds without seeming to register the pain. He held an automatic rifle by the barrel with his left hand, but the empty right was flailing desperately for balance while he tried to get his legs back under him despite the sucking peat. He was using the rifle as a clumsy walking stick, going for leverage, when Bolan leaned in close and shot him point-blank in the face, putting him down one final time.

A couple of the militiamen had him spotted, one already lining up a shot while his companion started calling to some others, pointing. Bolan wasn't sure how many of the squad were still alive, but he didn't intend to have the game reversed on him, become the hunted in another deadly game of hide-and-seek across the Everglades.

He took the gunman with the rifle at his shoulder first, since he was easily the greater threat. A 3-round burst from Bolan's SMG stitched across his gut, an inch or two above his belt, and spoiled the shooter's aim. Bent double at the waist, he fired straight down into the murky water as he collapsed.

That left his partner, raising the alarm, and Bolan swung to catch him with another silenced burst, his bullets tearing in beneath the arm that had been raised to point him out. The soldier's hoarse cries of alarm were cut off by a final, dying squawk from ruptured lungs.

Too late.

The others, four of them that he could see, all had a fix on Bolan now. One of the soldiers took off running in the opposite direction, churning water as he tried in vain for speed, while the other three were lining up their shots. They were too far apart for the Executioner to take all of them with one burst from his SMG, but he nailed one of them—the nearest shooter, on his left—before he plunged into the saw grass, dropping out of sight.

That didn't stop Bolan's enemies from firing, but they had to guess approximately where he was. With bullets whipping through the saw grass overhead, the movement caused by Bolan's passage was somewhat obscured. The shooters took no chances, firing high and low, unloading everything they had, but that kind of extravagance was hazardous with modern automatic weapons, where the largest magazine ran dry in seconds flat.

There came a sudden lull, and Bolan heard one of his adversaries cursing as he fumbled a replacement magazine out of its pouch. The other could be faking, standing ready with his weapon poised and loaded, but the Executioner would have to take that chance.

He popped up from the saw grass, thirty feet or so from where the riflemen had seen him last. The sudden movement caught one shooter's eye, but the other was glaring at his rifle while he tried to put the clip in backward, rattled by the proximity of death. The more alert commando was reloading, too, but making better time about it.

But it wasn't good enough.

The submachine gun stuttered, bullets ripping through the startled gunman's upper chest and shoulder, spinning him before he fell. The splash alerted his companion, who glanced up in time to lock eyes with his mortal enemy. His lips were moving, praying perhaps, but no sound came to Bolan's ears as he took up the trigger slack and finished it.

It was enough for now. He had two magazines remaining for the SMG before he had to switch to the Beretta, and he didn't feel like hunting humans in the Everglades with nothing but a side arm. He could still inflict grave casualties, but any soldier who deliberately entered battle without adequate supplies was foolish, asking to get killed.

Bone weary, still with too much work to do, he put the killing ground behind him and began backtracking toward the Zodiac inflatable.

7

Stone didn't panic when he heard the latest news from Virgil Blankenship. He *never* panicked, but he did decide that it was time for him to scrub his plans and split. He had done everything he could in preparation for the four-state raids, unless he went along to hold somebody's hand, and that had never been a part of the merc's design.

He understood that some of those who would go out on the coming raids would bungle their assignments, leaving clues behind for the police and FBI. It was entirely possible that some would be caught in the act, and under grilling, Stone was confident that they would crack, spill everything they knew.

That *was* part of the plan, unknown to members of the ASA. Stone had encouraged various attacks, including arson fires that had destroyed a number of black churches in the South, to pave the way for one night of coordinated raids that was a sure bet to nail headlines in the morning. At the same time, though, preceding acts of violence had potential targets on alert—and that was part of Stone's plan, too.

It was no good if all the night riders escaped. If Stone's employer simply wanted churches burned, the merc could have done the job himself or hired a torch for chicken feed. Instead, it was the nature of the crime, coupled with evidence that pointed to the far-right, racist fringe of U.S.

politics, that made the gig so profitable. When the smoke cleared on the morning after, liberal newscasters would beam their outrage to the farthest corners of the world, while victims of the raiding—the survivors, anyway—worked overtime to push new antiterrorism laws through Congress. At the same time, crackpots on the right would face indictments, trial and prison—maybe even execution, if they could be linked to a specific homicide—while Stone, Afif Rahman and Hezbollah were laughing up their sleeves.

It made no difference to the plan if Stone bailed out today, tomorrow or the next day. It was all on automatic pilot now. The time had come for the merc to save himself.

But first, he had to call Rahman.

It was the part he dreaded most, trying to make himself look brave, professional, while he informed Rahman that he was fleeing for his life. Of course, Stone wouldn't phrase it that way. He would tell the Arab what he knew about the two most recent skirmishes in Florida, explain that different factions of the ASA still had sufficient manpower to go ahead on schedule with the raids. Stone was convinced that the attacks in Florida were aimed at him specifically; he would have bet his life that Belasko was behind the sudden violence, either acting on his own or with the help of others. Stone had no idea who was behind Belasko, but it hardly mattered now. If he could slip away, unseen in the confusion, he still had a chance.

Rahman had been preparing for this day, had a secure retreat for Chris Stone and himself, where they could hide out if the deal went sour, or when the final chain reaction had begun to rip across the black belt of the Southern states. Their reservations were confirmed, and while Stone would have liked to make the journey by himself, he still needed Rahman to open certain doors along the way.

But not much longer. Once he had confirmed the last deposit to his numbered bank account, he would be parting company with Hezbollah forever. Let the Feds indict him if they ever got sufficient evidence. By that time, he would be a fading memory, and no one would survive to tell the FBI or ATF where he had gone.

He stood with one hand on the telephone, not lifting the receiver yet, rehearsing what he had to say. The truth might be annoying to Rahman, but it was far more dangerous to lie and later be found out. He would explain that someone still pursued him—that the wisest course of action was to leave, but he would also reassure Rahman that nothing would prevent the raids from going down on schedule. If Belasko and his backers knew about the plan, they would be striking all over the map, instead of trailing Stone from Baja to south Florida.

That made it something personal, and while he didn't have a clue what was behind the grim vendetta, Stone preferred to deal with adversaries one-on-one. He would have liked to kill Belasko, but at the moment he was more intent on bailing out, collecting what the Arabs owed him, getting started on a life of ease and luxury.

Once he was finished dealing with Rahman, Stone reckoned that he had an eighty-twenty shot at a successful getaway. It was a fact of life that anyone on earth could be located if the searchers had sufficient time and cash to spend, but Stone had been preparing for his final disappearance over several years. He had the paperwork lined up for several new identities; he had—or would have—all the money that he needed to retire in style. Without someone to finger Stone, it could take years to find him. Maybe decades. And if someone came to see him uninvited somewhere down the road, well, he would deal with that problem when it arose.

He lifted the receiver to his ear, tapped out the number he had memorized and waited through four rings for the familiar voice to answer.

"Yes?"

"We need to talk," Stone said.

THE WORLD HAD GONE to hell for Virgil Blankenship, but life went on. His lawyer's office was a block off Broward Boulevard, in Melrose Park, and Blankenship made sure that no one tailed him when he made the trip. Two hours had passed since he heard about the slaughter in the Glades, and there was nothing he could do to help those boys, but there was still a chance that he could help himself.

The lawyer's name was Reese, a good ol' boy whose heart was in the right place when it came to handling "special" cases for the Paul Revere Militia and the Klan. He charged a hundred bucks per hour on most clients, but the fee was cut by half for people he admired, the Christian soldiers who were working overtime to save their country from the strangling grip of ZOG.

Today, since there were still no charges pending and the law, from all appearances, was ignorant of what had happened in the Glades the past several days, Reese told his client to relax, clean up the mess as best he could and be discreet about it. If the Feds or local cops got after him, Blankenship should keep his mouth shut, make his phone call and let Reese deal with his problems in the courts. For now, though, it seemed possible that no one would report the killings in the swamp. Some of the dead would be removed by their surviving comrades, maybe planted elsewhere secretly; those who remained where they had fallen would be meat for scavengers, reduced to little more than rat-gnawed bones within a day or two. Some of them would be missed at home, or from their jobs, but that was someone else's problem. Blankenship sympathized, of course, but there was only so much he could do.

He had a small apartment in Virginia Gardens, where he got his mail and spent most nights when he wasn't involved in business for the Paul Reveres. He checked around the parking lot as he pulled in, made sure to lock his pickup, keeping one hand in his pocket near the Browning automatic that was tucked inside his waistband, underneath the loose tail of his shirt. Some kids were splashing in the pool as he went by, but they ignored him, and he returned the favor. His neighbors were mostly white trash, but they kept to themselves, without pestering him, and he liked it that way.

Blankenship started to relax a little as his key turned in the lock. He closed the door behind him, double locked it and was reaching for the light switch when he felt cold steel against his skull behind one ear.

"Think twice before you try to be a hero," someone said.

"It's cool," Blankenship replied, silently cursing at the tremor in his voice.

"Your first thought will be whether you should try the gun," his uninvited visitor went on. "It's your call, but the odds look poor from where I stand."

"No problem." The militiaman offered no resistance as a hand retrieved the Browning from its hiding place.

"That's it?"

"I only brought the one," he answered truthfully. There was no need to mention that he had a loaded Uzi in the bedroom for emergencies, or that he kept a riot shotgun in the closet, less than twenty feet away. The way things stood right now, it might as well have been a mile.

"Turn on the lights and have a seat."

The pistol was withdrawn, and Blankenship did as he was told. The gunman was a stranger to him, over six feet tall, perhaps two hundred pounds, dark hair, a face that told you he meant business. He saw that the stranger's Beretta had a sound suppressor attached, and that was bad. It meant the guy wasn't a cop, and that he might not mind if he was forced to shoot.

The sway-backed couch felt like a pit as Blankenship settled in, but he was conscious of the .45 beneath the middle cushion, inches from his hand. "What do you want?" he asked.

"I'm looking for Chris Stone," the stranger said. "I missed him at your place two nights ago."

Before Blankenship could feel relieved, the last part of the gunman's statement made him stiffen up again. If this man had been one of those who blitzed his compound in the Glades, then the militiaman knew damn well that he was capable of killing. It would be that easy, one squeeze of the trigger, and the job was done. The .45 was cocked and locked, but he would have to get his hand beneath the cushion, pull it out again, release the safety, aim and fire. By that time, the anonymous intruder would have nailed him ten or fifteen times, no sweat.

"He isn't here."

"I can see that," the gunman replied. "For the record, I'm not playing games, and I don't have a lot of time to spare."

"I don't know where he is right now," Blankenship said. "I swear to God."

"Give it a shot."

"I think he's going to bail. You know, I didn't want

him here in the first place. The trouble he was having out west, there. Who needs that shit?''

"You've got it on your doorstep now."

"You're telling me? That's why I've been after him to leave, the past two days. And then, this afternoon he says he's taking my advice. Big deal, like he was doing me some kind of favor, now that it's too late."

"You're breathing," the stranger said. "It could still be worse."

"I hear you. Anyway, that's all I know."

The big guy frowned. "He didn't tell you where he's going?"

"Nope. I didn't ask him, neither. None of my beeswax, okay? The less I know about what's going on with Stone, the healthier I feel."

"A little knowledge," the stranger said.

"Huh?"

"It's a dangerous thing. Sometimes you know too much, but not enough. What can I tell you?" He lifted the Beretta as if he were sighting down the slide.

"Well, hey! Hold on a minute, there! He did say something."

"Ah."

"Not this time, but the day he got here. We were talking back and forth about the shit out west, and Stone, he mentioned going to the islands when he wrapped up somethin' he was workin' on."

"What islands?"

"Hell if I know," Blankenship replied. "That's all he said. Out west, if someone says 'the islands,' they'd most likely mean Hawaii. Hereabouts, they're usually talkin' the Bahamas or Jamaica, someplace down in there."

"It isn't much."

"It's all I got. If you want to blow my head off because

I don't know something, that's your call. I'm trying to be straight with you."

The tall man seemed to think about it for a moment, finally rising from his seat and moving toward the door, still keeping Blankenship covered all the way. "I'd rather not come back," he said.

"I'd rather that you didn't, too."

"But if you're lying to me…"

"No, I swear."

And he could have let it go at that, except his gonads wouldn't let him. His hand slid underneath the cushion, found the warm grip of the .45, its checkered stocks rough to the touch. He thumbed off the safety before he pulled the weapon free, using that moment when the stranger had to glance away from him to orient himself and reach the doorknob. Blankenship wasn't sure if it would be enough; he knew only that he was honor-bound to try.

He had the big Colt nearly level when the stranger caught some kind of movement from the corner of his eye, and the Beretta snorted at him, barely louder than a muffled sneeze. The bullet struck him like a hard punch to the upper chest, more pressure than what Blankenship would have called an outright pain, and slammed him back against the couch.

The black Beretta was aimed directly at his face, and Blankenship tried to scream before the lights went out, but something kept the sound from rising in his throat.

Too late, he thought. It was over.

AFIF RAHMAN COULDN'T decide if he was angry or relieved. He had been too long in the West, away from home, coordinating Chris Stone's work in the United States and Mexico. It would be good to have that task behind him, but only if he was successful. Otherwise…

Stone had assured him that there was no problem. Clearly that was open to interpretation, since the unknown enemy was still pursuing the man, still killing members of the Paul Revere Militia and affiliated right-wing groups. The fact that Stone himself was still alive seemed something of a miracle, considering the obvious efficiency of his opponents. Still, the plan he had described involved attacks in four states, executed simultaneously, and except for Florida, the men assigned to carry out those raids were still alive and well. Surveillance was another matter, if the FBI or other agencies were onto them, but Stone assured him that the mission was secure. "No sweat," he said, although Rahman imagined he could hear Stone sweating on the telephone.

The beauty of the plan—*his* plan as much as Stone's—was that it could succeed to some extent without a single bullet being fired, a solitary bomb exploding. Even if the FBI arrested everyone involved before they had a chance to act, the press would treat it as a major story. Nothing like it had been tried since Reconstruction in America, more than 120 years ago, when early Klansmen roamed at will across the beaten South, coordinating midnight raids on Union troops and carpetbaggers.

Rahman knew his history. He also knew how most Americans would take the news of right-wing racist plotters scheming to attack black churches, synagogues, the homes of famous ethnic leaders. Even without bloodshed, it would rival stories of the Oklahoma City bombing—which, when all was said and done, had been the work of two or three fanatics with a truckload of manure. Americans loved their conspiracies. The racist right would suffer grievous injury in the United States, but more importantly, the U.S. would suffer reams of bad publicity abroad. If Washington couldn't protect its own minorities from native fascists, then what business did it have dictating peace terms in the Middle East?

All things considered, then, Rahman was happy to be leaving. He wasn't so pleased to think that Stone would share his hideaway, however briefly, but it should turn out all right as long as no one followed him. And if they did, well, there were ways to deal with that, too.

Where they were going, an American couldn't expect cooperation from the law. In fact, Rahman and Stone were guaranteed protection, for a price. He trusted those who made that promise, since they had been well paid in advance and since they understood the jeopardy they would be facing if they let him down. The long arm of Hezbollah could always reach them, even in their island paradise. There was no hiding place, and holy warriors nursed a grudge beyond the grave.

Fifteen minutes after speaking to Chris Stone, Rahman was almost finished packing. He had always traveled light, beginning in the days when he wore everything he owned. More recently, though he was now a wealthy man by peasant standards in his homeland, he was still a modest dresser, shunning jewelry and a lavish wardrobe, and could fit everything he needed for a trip around the world into a single bag. He would be forced to leave his guns behind—no weapons on this flight—but others would be waiting for him when he disembarked.

And one way or another, he would have to deal with Stone.

It would be relatively simple to dispose of him once they had reached their destination. Dig a shallow grave, and use one of Hezbollah's computer experts to retrieve the money from Stone's numbered bank account. Such things were possible. And yet, the more he thought about it while he finished packing, Rahman wondered if he ought to let the mercenary live—a little while at least.

For one thing, Stone had done his job despite some unexpected setbacks of the gravest sort. He had performed well under fire, avoided capture by the FBI and execution by the man or men who hunted him. More to the point, the problems he had suffered in performance of his task for Hezbollah had actually produced more headlines than Rahman had hoped for when they started. From initial coverage in the newspapers, on CNN and network news, the furor had expanded to the point that black and Jewish groups were calling for the appointment of a special prosecutor to investigate militias in America, determine whether they were plotting genocide or a revolt against the government.

It was delicious, well worth every cent that Stone had coming on their contract. But it would be even better if Rahman wasn't required to pay.

Stone would be useless to them after this; that much was obvious to anyone with one eye in his head and half a brain. The mercenary would be hiding out until he died, unless he found a surgeon who could change his face dramatically and thereby give him a new start. The fingerprints would still be trouble, though. Not even skin grafts did the trick with prints, surprisingly. The subject's own prints kept on growing back, even when they were whittled to the bone or seared with acid. It was something of a miracle, in fact—and it was Chris Stone's problem all the way.

If he was of no more use to Hezbollah, it followed that there was no point in keeping him alive. Rahman considered killing him in the United States, but he was on his own, and it would cause no end of trouble for him if he missed Stone on the first attempt. Such treachery might even prompt the mercenary to surrender, tell his story to the government in trade for mercy. *That* would be disaster, and the weight of it would fall upon Afif Rahman.

Better to wait, he thought, until they reached the islands. There, he would have all the time he needed to devise a strategy and find helping hands to dig the grave.

Rahman was smiling as he closed and latched his suitcase. He was looking forward to his flight and what was waiting for him at the other end.

THE ISLANDS.

It could mean anything, from the Aleutians to the Philippines, although some prospects seemed more likely than others. Bolan had already ruled out Hawaii on principle, assuming that a savvy mercenary being hunted by the Feds wouldn't attempt to hide on U.S. soil. It was a small first step, admittedly, in covering a planet whose surface was speckled with innumerable tidbits of inhabited real estate.

The islands.

That was plural, which, at least in theory, allowed him to eliminate such unlikely prospects as Iceland, Madagascar and Tasmania. Still not much help, as he was left with several hundred island chains or archipelagoes around the world, some boasting scores of islands on their own.

Proximity, the simple matter of convenience, told Bolan that a fugitive from Florida who sought "the islands" would most likely head for the Caribbean, as Virgil Blankenship himself had guessed. Assuming that he ruled out Cuba, there was still a wealth of island hideouts in the area to choose from. Most of them, including the Bahamas and Jamaica, had been serving fugitives and pirates from the early days of exploration, and they kept up that tradition to the present day, ignoring active drug cartels and playing host to banks that laundered dirty money from three continents. A man could lose himself down there, all right, and yet it seemed a bit too close for comfort.

If it had been Bolan on the run, he would have looked for someplace with a bit more distance from his trackers, someplace where they wouldn't think to look for him. The vast Pacific teemed with islands, millions of square miles of blue water, speckled with countless island chains. Some of them were infamous as bloody battlegrounds of World War II, while others carried names that few Americans had ever heard.

The islands.

It was hopeless, Bolan realized, without some kind of lead to point him in the right direction. He could spend the rest of his life island hopping and never put a dent in the list of potential targets.

Reluctantly he started looking for a public telephone. He didn't like disturbing Hal Brognola with requests for help, but there appeared to be no option in his present circumstances. Every moment wasted gave his adversary more of a head start. Wherever Stone was going, he could be well on his way by now.

Driving past a gas station, he saw the phone booth off to one side, partly sheltered from the street, and pulled his rental car into the lot. The scrambler Bolan lifted from the glove compartment was roughly the size of a cigarette pack. It attached to the phone with alligator clips, and he tapped out Brognola's private number, waiting while it rang three times.

"Hello?"

"Looks like I blew it," Bolan said.

Brognola, at his desk in Washington, D.C., didn't sound overly concerned. "How's that?" he asked.

"Stone got away from me again. He's running."

"From Miami?" Brognola asked.

"Sixty-forty," Bolan said. A flight out of Miami International made sense, but Stone could just as easily have slipped out through Savannah, Jacksonville or the Keys.

"You don't know where he's going?"

"One clue," Bolan said. "He told a friend he might be heading for 'the islands.' Could mean anything."

"Caribbean?"

"That was my first thought, but it seems too obvious. Too close."

Brognola thought about it for a moment, then said, "I'll make some calls, see if the passport people can be any help. You have a number there?"

"I'll call you back," Bolan said.

"Better let me have an hour."

"Right."

He picked a fast-food restaurant at random, dawdling over burgers that reminded him of flavored cardboard and a bag of fries that burned his tongue. The prefab milkshake helped soothe the burn, then drove a spike of cold through Bolan's palate, up into his skull. The clientele were mostly teenagers who had grown up on junk food and mistook it for nutritious fare.

The meal took thirty minutes, and he spent the next half hour driving aimlessly, spotting a number of neglected public telephones. The one he chose, when it was time, was mounted on the side wall of a neighborhood convenience store. He took the scrambler with him, hooked it up and dialed.

"We may have something," Brognola said.

"Oh?"

"Passport control, Miami International. Turns out they run a video on people passing through. Some deal they have with Treasury and Customs. Anyway, I leaned on them a little, faxed them some mugs on Stone and we got lucky.''

"He was on the tape?"

"It's ninety-five percent," Brognola said. "Guy came through wearing shades, a cap. You can't see everything, but we enhanced it, made an overlay. If it's not him, we tagged a damn suspicious look-alike.''

"Okay." The ninety-five percent was good enough for Bolan. He would have to check it out in any case.

"The bad news is, he's gone," Brognola said. "Took off on Transatlantic number 815 at half-past noon. The good news is, we know he's traveling as Charles Steven.''

"Where was he going?" Bolan asked.

"The islands," Brognola replied, "just like you thought. He's got a pit stop in Johannesburg, and then he's off to the Seychelles.''

The Executioner was smiling without mirth. "Okay," he said. "Looks like I've got a plane to catch.''

8

It was another day in paradise for Ahriman Boulard. The temperature was already ninety-two degrees, and he was sweating through the stylish business suit he wore in place of the dress uniform that would identify him as a major in the Seychelles military. He wasn't exactly under cover, but the Seychelles minister of trade had issued orders that official uniforms shouldn't be worn when meeting "special guests" on their arrival in the capital. It might look bad, and there had been enough adverse publicity already, since the government announced its latest plan for boosting revenue.

In 1996, the small Republic of Seychelles had put out the welcome mat to fugitives from all around the world. Come one, come all, they would be graciously received and guaranteed freedom from extradition...if they came up with a modest payment of one million dollars in advance. It was a one-time-only fee that would entitle "special visitors" to full protection of the law, without in any way exempting them from normal taxes, fees and other costs of living.

At a glance, the Seychelles seemed ideal for such a plan. The archipelago included more than a hundred islands of varying sizes, with native inhabitants concentrated on three. A majority of the republic's seventy-five thousand inhabitants resided on Mahé, the largest island, with some twenty-three thousand crammed into the capital city of Victoria; most of the chain's other natives were found on Praslin and La Digue islands, leaving ninety-odd pieces of tropical real estate virtually deserted. A fugitive with money to burn could have his pick to retire in style.

Unfortunately for the island state's economy, the hoped-for rush of hunted men and women never came to pass. Certainly there were a few such special visitors around, but even they came to the Seychelles with reluctance, after blowing all their other options. Boulard had been surprised that there weren't more applicants, but it made sense, the more he thought about it. Members of the giant criminal cartels had so corrupted various police and politicians in the West, from Montreal and Bogotá to Moscow, that they seldom felt the need to run and hide. Dictators who were toppled from their thrones mostly wound up in the United States or Switzerland, depending on their politics. The *really* hunted men—mass murderers and terrorists—typically were strapped for funds or thought themselves invincible.

It was with tangled feelings, then, that Boulard turned out to greet not one, but two most special visitors within a single day. They weren't on the same flight, naturally, so he had time to kill between delivering the first to his hotel and waiting for the second to arrive. Since there were rarely any happenings of note in the Seychelles, unless a hurricane swept through or something ate one of the tourists who went scuba diving off the coast, his mind stayed focused on the men he was assigned to chaperon.

The first had been American, traveling with a passport that identified him as Charles Stevens. Boulard would have been pleased to wager five years' salary that that wasn't, in fact, the stranger's name, but he would find no takers for such bets. The only rules concerning fugitives were cash up front and total abstinence from any criminal behavior that would harm the Seychelles people or their government.

So far, the second rule had been no problem, since the handful of felons on hand were all white-collar criminals, retiring from the game with their embezzled money, stolen stocks and bonds, before their webs began to unravel. One of them, it was true, had been accused of murdering a business partner several years earlier, staging the scene to make it look like suicide, but that wasn't the kind of crime that threatened anyone in the Seychelles.

Unfortunately, Boulard thought, all that could change.

The morning's first arrival was a grim-looking American who traveled light, one bag, no smile. He was some kind of mercenary, Boulard had been advised by his superiors—and damn successful at it, too, if he could pay the government's cover charge in cash. Beyond that vague description of his trade, however, and the fact that he was patently American, Boulard knew nothing of the grim man's history. Such questions were discouraged in the interest of deniability, as if a group of wide-eyed innocents would spend one million dollars each to rent themselves an island hideaway where no one knew their names.

The second flight was fifteen minutes late, which qualified as punctual in the Seychelles. It was a small plane, seating twenty passengers, but only half that number were on board. Six of the ten were European tourists, three were Seychellois, and one—the last man off the plane—was clearly Arab.

He was the man Boulard had been dispatched to meet.

Boulard stepped up to greet his special guest. "Mr.

Rahman,'' he said in English, one of the republic's two official languages, ''welcome to the Seychelles.''

The handshake was abbreviated, firm and dry. The plane was air-conditioned, and it would be several seconds yet before the Arab started to sweat through his clothes. If he was from the Middle East, though, he should be accustomed to the heat, if not the tropical humidity that made ninety degrees Fahrenheit feel like one hundred and ten.

''I have an air-conditioned car,'' Boulard informed the man who might or might not be Afif Rahman. ''It is not far to your hotel. Tomorrow, or whenever you prefer, I will have residential listings for you to select—''

''A friend of mine was coming in ahead of me,'' the Arab interrupted him. ''Has he arrived?''

Boulard considered his reply. Questions weren't forbidden, in the strictest sense, but those who dealt with special visitors were constantly reminded that their guests had paid for privacy.

Boulard decided it was safer if he answered with a question of his own. ''Your friend would be…?''

''Charles Stevens,'' Rahman said. ''American, fair haired, athletic-looking. I believe he would have flown in from Johannesburg.''

Boulard relaxed. No one had told him that the new arrivals were associates, but he couldn't imagine any government or individual that would pay one million dollars in advance to find a fugitive. It would be wasted money, anyway, since extradition was impossible, and they were searched for weapons on arrival in Victoria.

''Your friend arrived this morning,'' Boulard said. ''In fact, it was my pleasure to escort him to the Hotel Marcellais, where you are also registered.''

Rahman seemed satisfied. At any rate, he spoke no

more as they proceeded to the baggage area and Boulard walked him through the mandatory customs check. Such things as drugs and weapons could be purchased in the capital, as anywhere, but special visitors were always cautioned not to carry contraband themselves. Rahman raised no objection to the search, and it was soon completed. Boulard summoned a porter to convey the Arab's bags to the Lincoln Towncar outside.

"In five minutes," he informed Rahman, "you can see your friend."

The Arab frowned and answered, "He can wait."

THE FLIGHT to Amsterdam departed from Miami International on time. Mack Bolan rode in business class, a compromise between the lush extravagance of first class and the muscle-cramping seats available in coach. From Amsterdam, he would be flying to Johannesburg, then picking up a shuttle flight from there to the Seychelles. With layovers in Amsterdam and Jo'burg, it would take more than a day to reach his destination, but for once he didn't chafe at the delay. No one was waiting for him at the other end, and he could use the time to plan what he should do once he arrived.

Bolan knew all about the Seychelles government's attempt to make the island chain a Mecca for affluent fugitives. The plan had drawn attention, not because it was unique, but rather for the openness with which the Seychellois declared their land an outlaw's haven. Other nations that had gone that route, from Mexico and Costa Rica to Algeria, traditionally kept up some pretense, however flimsy, that they were committed to the rule of law. It was the flagrant honesty of their *dis*honesty that set the Seychellois apart.

In concrete terms, that meant the men he hunted would

be under government protection from police, perhaps the military, such as it might be. He could expect the state to intervene once he began to make his move, and that posed special problems for the Executioner, but nothing that he hadn't dealt with in the past. Surprise was his advantage, knowing Stone wouldn't believe he had been traced to the Seychelles so soon.

A hotel room and rental car were waiting for him in Victoria. He also had the names and addresses of two men who could sell him arms and ammunition at a rate on par with street sales in New York. Once he was armed, he could begin the hunt.

One thing was troubling Bolan, though. Most of the loot from holdups executed in the States by the Paul Revere Militia was accounted for. Even allowing for the weapons trade with Mexico, which had been flourishing before Bolan arrived in Baja California, he still had trouble understanding where Chris Stone would get the cash required to buy himself a hideaway in the Seychelles. One possibility had dogged him since Brognola had informed him of the mercenary's destination, and it kept him from relaxing on the transatlantic flight.

Suppose Stone had another sponsor, someone who wasn't a member of the Paul Revere Militia? Who would it be? What motive lay behind his funding of domestic terrorism in the States? Who stood to benefit from right-wing violence directed at the government and various minorities?

That was the question Bolan would have to answer before he could complete his mission. It would be someone—or some state—with ample cash on hand, connections in the underworld of crime and terrorism, coupled with a desire to generate upheavals in America. The list wasn't exactly short, when nations as diverse as Cuba,

North Korea, Jordan and Liberia took turns defying the United States, trying to throw their weight around at home and overseas. Instead of disappearing in the 1980s, as some politicians claimed, the blight of terrorism had diversified, expanded from its regular haunts to plague the world at large. No longer was such violence confined to Palestinian guerrillas, Irish rebels or Basque gunmen in the Pyrenees. Wherever ethnic turmoil or religious rivalries existed, one side or another—and more often both—resorted to the tools of violence with a seeming disregard for human suffering. Increasingly the stain of sociopolitical mayhem was seen in the United States, as well.

Upset about your taxes? Bomb the nearest federal building. Angry at a minister for speaking out on the abortion issue, one way or another? Burn his church. Disgruntled that a presidential press conference preempted "Jeopardy"? Take your AK-47 to the White House, see if you can bag the Man.

It seemed insane, and Bolan had no doubt that some of those involved in the proliferation of such acts were certifiable, but he wasn't a shrink or social worker. It was comforting to sit around at cocktail parties and debate the roots of violence, while a waiter served smoked salmon and champagne, but empty talk had never solved a problem in the grim world Bolan occupied. The predators he dealt with were a breed apart, translating their desires to action, preying on the weak wherever they were found.

And when you stripped the rhetoric away, looked past the "holy" causes publicly espoused by every terrorist who ever drew a breath and aimed a gun, you saw that they were all alike. Left-wing or right, regardless of their race, religious creed or ethnic roots, all terrorists wanted the same thing.

Control.

He had picked up a guidebook on the Seychelles while he waited for his flight to board out of Miami, and he read it through while they were airborne. Most of what it told him was irrelevant to Bolan's mission, but he scanned it anyway. He knew, for instance, that fifty-nine percent of the Seychellois were city dwellers, ninety percent of them Roman Catholic, eighty-five percent literate. The islands had been uninhabited when Portuguese sailors discovered them in the early sixteenth century, and for the next two hundred years they served as little more than rest stops for marauding pirates. France claimed them in 1756, settling the chain with white planters and African slaves, and interbreeding did the rest. England took the archipelago away from France in 1814, and the Seychelles remained a British protectorate until full independence was granted in 1976. One-party rule was in effect until 1991 when opposition parties were legalized, and a new, more liberal constitution was adopted two years later. Now, it seemed, the Republic of Seychelles was taking a nostalgic turn back toward the pirate days, inviting exiled felons to drop by and put down roots.

So be it.

Bolan didn't judge his fellow men; they did that for themselves, by word and deed. In Bolan's mind, he was their judgment, visited upon them by a universe that finally cried "Enough!"

Judgment was on its way to the Seychelles.

A CENTIPEDE SIX INCHES long was scurrying around the bathtub, sliding back each time it tried to climb the walls of porcelain. Stone reckoned it had come up through the drainpipe and was too stupid to retrace its steps. He watched it for a moment, then turned on the shower, extrahot, and sluiced it down the drain. After he shut off the water, he found the rubber plug and jammed it into place, preventing any other visitors from coming in that way.

"Four star, my ass."

The hotel room was adequate, but nothing to write home about. He was relieved to be out of the States, to leave the heat behind, but Stone didn't intend to spend his life in the Republic of Seychelles. It was a tourist trap, for one thing; he could never rest assured that some American wouldn't drop by and recognize his face from CNN or *Newsweek,* after all the chaos and the bad publicity that he had left behind. No Feds could reach him here, but Stone didn't enjoy the thought of being cornered, either. It evoked a claustrophobic feeling in his gut that made him want to scream.

A month or two—no more than six—and he would slip away. If anybody asked where he was going, Stone would tell them he had business to take care off. He'd leave most of his things behind, just for appearances, and split with what could fit into a briefcase: passports, credit cards, his bankbooks.

Rahman had talked him into visiting the Seychelles, giving it a shot. Stone knew about the sanctuary program and had balked at shelling out a million dollars for the privilege of lying low, but then the Arab had said that *he* was picking up the tab, a kind of bonus for the work Stone had accomplished in the States. That kind of generosity evoked immediate suspicion, but the mercenary knew enough to watch his back. It would be safer, he decided, if they met on neutral ground, as long as he could keep Rahman in sight.

Four hours in the country, and he had already armed himself. The two Browning semiauto pistols were nothing much despite the hefty price, but they would do while he was waiting for delivery on the other hardware he had ordered. By the following morning, he would have an Uzi submachine gun and enough 9 mm parabellum ammunition to defend himself against all comers.

Not that Stone had any reason to believe Rahman meant to dispose of him in the Seychelles. He wouldn't put it past the Arab, but there had been nothing in Rahman's demeanor to suggest an active plot at work. Rather, Stone made a point of taking extra care no matter where he was or with whom he was dealing. Certainly his several brushes with the Reaper in the past two weeks had honed his paranoia to a razor's edge.

He checked his watch against the wall clock, noting that Rahman should be arriving soon. Stone hadn't raised the subject of his final payment while they were preparing to depart from the United States, but he didn't intend to let the Seychelles cover charge wipe out the money he was owed from Hezbollah. It would be pushing matters to request a bonus, granted, but he meant to pocket every penny he had coming. If Rahman tried holding out on him, the terrorist would quickly learn what real terror was about.

Stone scanned the skyline of Victoria through tinted window glass and was grateful for air-conditioning. Sometimes it seemed that he had spent his whole life sweating since he joined the Army and was sent away to boot camp, followed by the Special Forces jump school at Fort Benning. Still, the tropic heat was better than a blizzard, and besides, the cooler climates found in North America and Europe would be out-of-bounds for years to come while he was being hunted by the FBI and Interpol.

His own reflection in the windowpane was ghostly, staring back at him with lifeless eyes. He thought about the prospect of revising his appearance, shopping for an able surgeon who could change his nose, chin, eyes—hell, anything he wanted changed, to make himself a brand-new man. Invisible. It would be costly, but if it could save his life and keep the hunters off his back, it would be worth the price.

He thought again about retirement, trying the concept on for size, and found that he couldn't imagine sitting idle for the next three decades, fishing, basking in the sun, beachcombing, getting laid from time to time. With a new face, he could go back to work, at least part-time, selective hits for wealthy clients who could easily afford the best. Afif Rahman and Hezbollah might even have some use for him, if Stone thought he could trust the Arabs with the knowledge of his new existence.

Wait and see.

Stone had a tendency to plan so far ahead sometimes that he lost sight of more immediate concerns. It was a weakness he controlled through constant vigilance and practice, through a force of will. Today, right now, he had to concentrate on getting paid. Beyond that point, he would be staying in the Seychelles long enough to give himself some breathing room.

After that, the big picture would take care of itself.

The telephone beside his bed rang with a funny chirping sound, as if a bird were trapped inside. Stone crossed the room and lifted the receiver, knowing it could only be one person in the world.

''Hello.''

"Are you available for drinks in half an hour?" Afif Rahman asked. "There is a lounge downstairs."

"I'll be there," Stone replied, and heard a click before the dial tone started humming in his ear.

It gave him time to triple-check the Brownings and decide which one he ought to carry with him to the meeting. On second thought, perhaps he ought to carry both. Rahman would hardly try to waste him in the Hotel Marcellais, but then again, he might be counting on that kind of logic to make Stone let down his guard.

He would take both guns. Just in case.

AFIF RAHMAN HAD HAD a long and uneventful flight from the United States. His greeting at the airport had been all that he could hope for in the circumstances, but he didn't feel at home in the Seychelles.

In truth, he felt at home nowhere. His people had been driven out of Palestine by the United Nations to accommodate the Jews some fifteen years before Rahman was born. His father and his older brother had been *fedayeen* with Al-Fatah, before the traitor Arafat had turned to making peace with the eternal enemy. His father had been killed by the Israelis on a border raid. His brother was shot down in Jordan when the faithless monarchy had launched a civil war against the Palestinians, spilled Arab blood to pacify rich Jews in the United States. Rahman suspected that he wouldn't recognize his homeland now if God handed him the deed.

But still, he fought.

For some men, for some nations, fighting was a way of life. The cause may change or even be forgotten, but the war went on. Too much blood had been spilled along the way for Hezbollah to live in peace on any terms but total victory. The day the last Jew died in Palestine, Afif Rahman would think about retiring from the fight.

And even then, he wasn't sure if he could lay his weapons down.

There were so many other enemies, besides the Zionists. America and most of Western Europe sided with the Jews against the Palestinians. Those nations and their people had to be punished for that crime. The so-called Arab leaders who had lost their way and sanctioned peace with Israel had to be weeded out and executed as examples to the rest. Those countries that maintained a neutral stance were equally at fault, for standing idle while Israel and the United States committed genocide against the rightful heirs to Palestine.

Rahman wasn't disheartened by the thought that he would be at war until the day he died. In fact, it gave him purpose, offered him a strange sense of stability that weaker men didn't possess. It was a comfort knowing how he would be spending the remainder of his days. It made him proud to know that his last breath would be spent cursing the Israelis and the American scum who aided them.

But first, there was Chris Stone.

Rahman could make a case that Stone hadn't fulfilled their contract to the letter, but he didn't feel like being petty. Stone had caused considerable turmoil in America, and more was coming if his cronies in the so-called Secret Army carried out their raids on schedule. Rahman wished there had been more Jews among the dead, but even dead militiamen were dead Americans, and that was all that counted in the long run. Every drop of blood spilled in the States was partial payment for lives lost in sacred Palestine.

But it would never be enough.

Rahman considered killing Stone himself, but worried that the mercenary might be ready for him, half expecting treachery. A wiser move would be to stay in Stone's good graces, pay him as agreed and keep in touch with him for future work, until a hunting party could be fielded to destroy him. After that, retrieval of the money from his numbered bank account would be a bland computer exercise, child's play.

Stone had been useful, but he had no loyalty to the cause of Palestine. It was too much for him, or any other American, to expect fair treatment from the people they had robbed and murdered over half a century. As long as Stone was fool enough to serve his mortal enemies for pay, so be it, but his ultimate reward would still be death.

Rahman glanced at his watch and saw that he had ten minutes left before his rendezvous with Stone. He would defer unpacking until he returned.

The weapons had been waiting for him when he got to the hotel. Rahman's advance man had been busy in the Seychelles for two days, preparing for his master to arrive. A submachine gun and a semiautomatic pistol, both Berettas, lay together on his bed, beside the duffel bag that held spare magazines and ammunition. If he needed help, his backup was available, prepared to move in moments at a signal from Rahman.

He put the SMG back in the duffel bag and zipped it, slid it underneath the bed and out of sight. The pistol fit quite nicely underneath his belt, in back where it would be completely hidden by his sport coat.

Perfect.

There would be no shooting in the cocktail lounge, if he could help it, but soldiers always had to be prepared.

Feeling a sudden gladness, Rahman left his room and locked the door behind him, moving toward the elevators and his meeting with Stone.

9

The guns were easy. Bolan had been supplied with names of two arms dealers, passed along to Hal Brognola from the CIA, and all the cash he needed to acquire a mini-arsenal. The dealer he selected had a pawnshop on the south side of Victoria and kept his stock of weapons in a fire-resistant vault with double combination locks. There was no dickering on price, and dollars were acceptable in place of rupees.

When Bolan left the shop, he felt prepared to tackle anything that might come up in the Seychelles. One OD duffel bag contained the weapons he had purchased, while a second held the ammunition and explosives. A new Beretta Model 92-S hung beneath his arm in fast-draw leather, and a sound suppressor to fit the side arm was included in the deal.

An hour later, Bolan stood atop the roof of a twelve-story office building in downtown Victoria and gazed across the boulevard at another building some fifty paces distant. He was checking out the next floor to the top, where slightly tinted windows let him pick out moving shapes behind the glass.

After a moment, he knelt, removed a newly purchased sniper rifle from the duffel at his feet and opened up the folding wooden stock. The piece was an Israeli Galil, chambered in 7.62 mm and fitted with a Nimrod telescopic scope, designed to score head shots at any range up to 300 meters, with a guarantee, in skillful hands, of upper-body hits at twice that range. A semiautomatic weapon, the Galil featured a folding bipod and held twenty rounds in its detachable box magazine. With the suppressor snug in place, its barrel measured twenty-seven inches overall.

He scanned the target window, left to right and back again, first counting heads, then studying the faces. There were four men in the room, but Bolan wanted only one of them. The others were unknown to him, presumably employees or associates of the man he intended to kill. His mark would be the one behind the massive desk, smoking a fat cigar and talking with his hands.

René Bruton ranked eighth or ninth among the richest men in the Republic of Seychelles. Ostensibly his fortune came from copra, and indeed, his family had been doing very well in the business for several generations. Lately, though, Bruton had taken it upon himself to broaden the horizons of the family business to include cocaine and heroin. He stayed in business and remained at liberty thanks to connections with the same government that had decided it would be a good idea to welcome foreign fugitives as paying guests. Around election time, Bruton was known for generosity to both established parties, and he always had a list of well-placed friends in government.

It was an easy shot, compared to some that the Executioner had made. The thick glass might deflect his first round, but that still left nineteen in the magazine, and Bolan had no doubt that two or three would be enough to do the job. He found Bruton's bland profile in the Nimrod's lens and placed the crosshairs on his temple, just above the pockmarked cheek. Up close and personal, a blue swirl of cigar smoke looked like tule fog.

Bruton was in midsentence when the first round drilled his window. He was startled by the popping sound and had started turning toward the window when the bullet, jogged off target, struck him in the upper chest. The impact rocked him in his swivel chair, and he was gasping in surprise when the second round flew in past open lips, cored through the juncture of his spinal cord and skull, nearly decapitating Bruton where he sat.

The others were recoiling, one guy doubled over, vomiting onto his shoes, as Bolan swiveled to his right and fired off three more rounds. He aimed above their heads, preferring witnesses to corpses at the moment, bringing down the window in a rain of jagged splinters, drilling clean holes in the walls. Across the street, he could hear one of the survivors calling out for help. A twenty-something secretary stuck her head into the room, got one look at her boss and started to scream.

Bolan packed up the rifle, left his scattered brass to mark the spot and drew a folded piece of paper from the duffel bag. He left it on the roof and used an empty shell casing to weight it down. Whoever opened it would find a mug shot of Chris Stone, his name and physical description printed underneath, together with a message: "Give him up."

Bolan had no idea if it would work, but it was bound to light a fire under the fugitive. And in the process, it might also lead him to Stone's contact, still a faceless cipher. Bolan wanted him—or them—as well, but as he put the rooftop sniper's post behind him, he could almost hear Mick Jagger telling him, "You can't always get what you want."

"But if you try sometimes," the Executioner stated, "you get what you need."

GASTON DALADIER WASN'T a man to worry over trifles. He was sixty-two years old and had survived a bout with cancer, not to mention two divorces and innumerable plots by his competitors to drive him out of business. He was still around, however, and the men who tried to break him had themselves been broken. He didn't scare easily, but he was troubled now.

Not frightened—that would be too strong a term. No, *troubled* fit his mood precisely as he paced his study, waiting for the telephone to ring. A full half hour had elapsed since he had heard the news about René Bruton, the unknown gunman who had killed him and the message that was left behind. Daladier had ordered an immediate inquiry to discover what the message meant, and he was waiting for an answer now, impatient, chafing at the delay.

Daladier had earned his first two million dollars in the import-export business, trading cinnamon and copra for the manufactured goods the Seychellois required in order to survive. Man couldn't live on fish and coconuts alone, and with the money earned from tourism, his people rushed to buy imported food and clothes, appliances, vehicles, power tools—most anything, in fact, that could not readily be grown or manufactured on a string of tiny coral atolls. In time, Daladier's wealth and friendship with the best and brightest in Victoria had landed him the job as deputy assistant minister of commerce. The title brought a meager salary, which he was glad to waive, thus earning kudos in the press for his devotion to the common good. It also let him take a cut of two percent from every load of contraband that reached the islands, whether drugs or weapons, smuggled alcohol or cigarettes, black-market medicine or pornography. Whatever could be sold illegally to tourists or the native Seychellois, Gaston Daladier would have a finger in the pie.

He had been René Bruton's friend for many years, a silent partner in the shipment of narcotics to the islands, and now he worried that the Seychelles might be about to face a gang war for control of the illicit trade. It was unthinkable, considering the steps the government had taken to monopolize such traffic. Still...

The jangling telephone made him jump, and he bit off a curse as he turned to pick up the receiver. *"Oui?"*

"Mr. Daladier?" He recognized the voice at once: his contact with the capital police.

"Who else were you expecting?"

"Um, ah, that is, sir, I have the information you require."

"Then give it to me."

He listened to the officer for ninety seconds, memorizing everything he heard. It was a talent he had cultivated as a child, and it had served him well throughout his life. When the policeman finished his report, Daladier asked three short questions.

"Did he come alone?"

"Yes, sir," the officer replied, "but he was joined some hours later by another man. A Palestinian, apparently. He calls himself Afif Rahman."

"Where are they now?"

"The Hotel Marcellais, sir."

"Who is their chaperon?"

"A Major Ahriman Boulard."

Daladier hung up without another word. His mind was racing, sifting through potential steps that he could take to minimize the problem that confronted him. The first thing he would have to do was speak to his immediate superior and thereby demonstrate that he was in control. Whatever action he decided on from there would need approval from upstairs in any case.

He pressed a button on the desktop intercom and stood waiting as the butler stepped into his study. "I require the car immediately."

"Yes, sir."

Two minutes later, when his servant came back to inform him that the limousine was waiting at his door, Daladier went out to meet the car. The butler trailed him through the house, but didn't cross the threshold, where a bodyguard stood waiting for him.

There was little violent crime in the Seychelles, but men of wealth and influence brought out the worst in the lower classes. Until now, Daladier had viewed his team of private gunmen almost as a status symbol rather than a matter of necessity, but that had changed since he received the news about René Bruton.

The bodyguard moved out in front of him, the jacket of his suit unbuttoned so that he could reach the pistol slung beneath his arm. He opened the limousine's door for Daladier, held it with one hand while he scanned the street in each direction. There was normal traffic, nothing out of place.

Daladier was stooping to enter the car when it happened. He heard a smack, as if someone had slapped his bodyguard across the face, and some warm liquid splattered on his cheek. The minister brought up a hand to wipe it off, already turning toward the young man, blinking at the body stretched out on the pavement. Blood was streaming from the gunman's shattered skull. Daladier saw crimson on his own fingers, realizing that he had caught a portion of the spray.

When the bullet struck Daladier, it jerked him backward, off his feet and slammed him to the pavement. He was dazed, aware of pressure on the upper quadrant of his chest, but no real pain yet. More blood soaked through his shirt and jacket, *his* blood, and no matter how he tried, he found that he couldn't stand up.

"Ah, *merde*." He mouthed the curse with no great ardor, lying on his back and staring at the sky above him, brilliant blue, without a trace of clouds. But it was darkening, he saw. How was that possible, so early in the day? There had been no reports of an eclipse. Daladier would definitely have remembered that.

Too late he understood. The faces bending over him were curious, detached from his private tragedy.

He heaved a final sigh and let the darkness carry him away.

STONE WAS CONSIDERING a long walk through the city just to see the sights, maybe pick up the Uzi, when he was distracted by the telephone. His frown was automatic, a reflexive action. Only a few people knew where he was, and none of them had any business calling him unless they were delivering bad news. Tempted to let it slide, Stone knew it would be reckless of him to ignore the call, and so he reluctantly lifted the receiver.

"Yes?"

"Hello, please, Mr. Stevens?"

"Speaking."

"I am Ahriman Boulard. You may remember that I met you at the airport?"

Stupid bastard. It had only been four hours since they parted company. He had to think Stone was an idiot.

"Yes, I remember you."

"It is important that I speak with you," Boulard went on.

"Okay."

"If it would be possible for us to speak in person...?"

"I was going for a walk," Stone said.

"The matter is important, I assure you."

"Yeah, okay. I'll meet you somewhere."

"I am in the lobby, as it happens," Boulard said. "Perhaps we should discuss this matter first, before you leave the Marcellais."

Stone hesitated, frowning. What could it be? If this creep planned on touching him for extra cash, he had a king-size disappointment coming.

"Okay," he said. "Come up. We'll talk."

"Thank you. A moment, if you please."

The line went dead, and Stone hung up the telephone. He drew the Browning automatic from his waistband, double-checked the live round in the chamber, pulled the loaded magazine, then put it back. He had no reason to believe that Ahriman Boulard was any threat, and even if he tried some kind of strong-arm play, the gun would have to be a last resort. Stone would be up the creek without a paddle if he started cranking off rounds in the Hotel Marcellais. This wasn't Idaho, or even Baja, where a man could sometimes get away with that. He was a stranger here, and there was no way off the island if he started drawing heat.

No shooting, then, unless his life was clearly on the line.

He was standing in the middle of the room and waiting when he heard footsteps approaching in the corridor outside. There was a soft knock on his door, and Stone put one eye to the peephole, turning left and right to let the fish-eye lens convince him that Boulard didn't have company. When he was satisfied, the merc opened the door and waved his visitor inside.

"Something to drink?" he asked.

"No, thank you. I cannot stay long. This business is most upsetting."

"What exactly *is* the problem?" Stone inquired.

"There have been...incidents...within the past two hours," Boulard said.

"What kind of incidents?"

"Shootings, sir. Lives have been lost."

"Well, hey, if you're accusing me—"

"No, no." Boulard held up one hand as if he were about to take an oath in court. "We know that you are not responsible for these audacious crimes. And yet, you *are* involved."

"How's that?"

Boulard lowered his hand and reached inside his jacket. Stone was braced to rush him if he came out with a weapon, but instead he drew a folded piece of paper and stepped forward, handing it to Stone.

"What's this," the mercenary asked, "another bill?"

"Please open it, sir."

Stone did as he was asked and felt the smile drop from his face. He stared into his own eyes, grainy black-and-white but readily identifiable. He saw that a detailed description had been printed beside the photo, not unlike the standard Wanted posters that you saw in the United States. It was the last line, though, printed across the bottom of the page, that tied his gut in knots. There were three little words, a simple message: "Give him up."

"Is this supposed to be some kind of joke?" Stone crumpled the paper in his fist and squeezed it hard enough to make his knuckles crack.

"I can assure you, we are not amused, sir." Boulard stood firm. "There have been several attacks. Four men are dead, one wounded. At each place, one of these papers was retrieved."

"You mean to say somebody's hunting me?"

"It would appear so," Boulard said. "Two of the people killed were wealthy, influential men. One was a simple bodyguard. The last one…''

''What?''

''He was a special visitor to the republic, like yourself.''

''He was a fugitive, you mean.''

''I do not judge, sir. An Englishman, he was, who made arrangements similar to yours.''

''I don't know any Englishmen in the Seychelles,'' Stone said. ''I don't know anyone, for Christ's sake!''

''I am not implying that the man was killed because you knew him. The targets, I believe, were chosen as a demonstration, to instruct us that the man or men responsible can reach whomever he—or they—desire.''

''So, what's the bottom line on this?'' Stone asked.

''The bottom line, sir?''

''The skinny, pal, all right? Your people got their cash up front to guarantee that I wouldn't be bothered. Now you come around and show me this—'' he tossed the wadded paper back at Boulard, and bounced it off his chest ''—like I'm supposed to save *your* ass or something. What's the deal?''

''I thought you should be made aware that there is danger for you in the city.''

''Listen, if you can't take care of something like this for a million bucks—''

''The price is not an issue,'' Boulard said, a certain stiffness in his tone suggesting that he might have been offended. ''You are under my protection here for the duration of your stay.''

''And what about the limey?'' Stone inquired.

''The what?''

''The Englishman! Were you protecting *him?*''

''He had been here for some time,'' Boulard replied.

"There were no threats against him, and surveillance had become—how shall I say?—relaxed."

"I see. May I assume that you won't be relaxing on *my* case?"

"Indeed, sir. You are as safe as · in your mother's arms."

"You never met my mother," Stone replied.

THE GRENADES WERE Russian RGD-5 models, with percussion fuses connected to 110 grams of TNT. The egg-shaped, apple green steel casings had serrated linings, thus designed to fragment when they detonated, spewing deadly shrapnel for a radius of twenty yards. Once Bolan pulled the safety pin, he would have 4.2 seconds in which to deliver his pitch, then get out of the way.

Each grenade weighed eleven ounces, and the Executioner had four of them clipped to his belt as he stepped out of the rental car, parked half a block due north of his intended target. Extra weight was added by the MP-5 K submachine gun tucked beneath his right arm, clasped against his side, and the Beretta semiauto pistol underneath his left.

The Executioner was dressed to kill.

His target was a warehouse on the outskirts of Victoria, where recently imported merchandise was stored before it made its way to shops throughout the capital. At different times, the place was known to handle clothing, canned goods and electrical appliances. It also unofficially stored hashish, heroin, cocaine and weapons banned by law in the Republic of Seychelles. On any given day, a hundred kilograms of coke might occupy a crate next door to beans and franks from England or machine parts from South Africa.

The owner was a Seychellois named Anton Mayer. According to the DEA and Interpol, he was a bosom buddy of the Cali cartel, as well as poppy growers in the Golden Crescent, which included Turkey and Iran. It didn't trouble him that most of his own countrymen averaged six thousand dollars per year in real income, or that some of them were kicking back forty percent of that, on average, to support drug habits. It was rumored that Mayer's drug connections had begun in casual conversation with a fugitive from Western justice, living in Victoria, but Bolan didn't care much one way or the other.

He was looking for a mark, and this would do.

Three cars were parked outside the warehouse, one a shiny BMW, the others showing signs of wear and tear. He mounted concrete steps to reach the loading dock and tried the access door, but found it locked.

No sweat.

He drew the MP-5 K, with its sound suppressor attached, and fired three rounds into the locking mechanism of the door. A heartbeat later, he was standing in a corridor with one light bulb suspended from the ceiling, roughly halfway along. It wasn't dark, though, since the warehouse lights were blazing at the far end of the hallway, guiding Bolan in.

Apparently no one had heard him blow the lock. When Bolan reached the warehouse proper, he found two men operating forklifts, while three others huddled in an open office to his right. He moved in that direction first, one man glancing up as he approached and staring as if he had seen a ghost. He tried to warn the others, but he came up tongue-tied, stammering.

The man in charge still had his back turned when Death stepped into the office doorway. Finally, too late, he turned to find out what his friend was gaping at, and it was his turn to go bug-eyed, gaping at the new arrival

and the submachine gun in his hands. The three men had
been speaking French when Bolan entered, but the leader
switched to English.

"Is this a robbery?" he asked. The very concept
seemed to dazzle him.

"Not quite," the Executioner replied, and fired a
3-round burst into his chest. The dead man tumbled backward, sprawling across his desk before the others understood exactly what was happening.

The man on Bolan's left was carrying a side arm, and
he tried to reach it, digging underneath the loose tail of
his shirt, but the attempt was much too little, far too late.
The MP-5 K whispered to him, parabellum shockers slamming him against a nearby file cabinet, his body slumping
to the floor as if his bones had turned to mush.

The lone survivor had his hands raised in surrender,
begging for his life while tears streamed down his cheeks.
It could have been an act, and Bolan wasn't taking any
chances.

"Take your shirt off," he demanded, and the smaller
man obeyed so zealously that he sent buttons pattering
across the floor. He seemed to be unarmed, and while an
ankle holster was remotely possible, Bolan was willing to
assume the risk.

"Come here."

The trembler approached Bolan, stood before him like
a supplicant in church. The warrior half turned to face the
storage area and nodded toward the two men on the
forklifts.

"Are they armed?" he asked.

"No, sir."

"All right, then. You go fetch them, and get out of
here. You understand?"

"Get out?" There was a sudden glint of hope behind those eyes. "Of course! As you command!"

"And take this with you," Bolan said, delivering a folded piece of paper to the other's trembling hand. "Give it to the police, all right?"

"Yes!" The guy was anxious to be anywhere but standing in the presence of a maniac who spoke in riddles. "I will do as you have said."

"So split."

He waited, watched the shirtless man run shouting toward the forklift operators, speaking to them hurriedly. The others glanced Bolan's way before all three evacuated through a side door. Gone.

How long would it be before they found a telephone and spoke with the police? There was no telling, but he took the time to walk along the rows of crated merchandise, quickly examining it, pausing when he saw a double row of metal canisters painted bright fire-engine red.

Acetylene.

He palmed one of the Russian frag grenades, retreating toward the nearest exit as he pulled the pin, wound up and made his pitch. Bolan was halfway to the loading dock before it blew, the first blast nothing in comparison to what came afterward, the red tanks blowing one after the other like a string of giant firecrackers.

Not bad.

Bolan allowed himself a smile when he was seated in his rental car.

Not bad at all.

But he was only getting started in Victoria. The locals and their treasured special guests still had a lot to learn about the Executioner.

10

No matter how he focused, Ahriman Boulard couldn't recall a worse day in his thirty-seven years of life. At one time or another, he had lived in poverty, had watched his younger brother die from an infected spider bite, had suffered from malaria himself and had survived his military basic training under officers who made the course a living hell on earth. But nothing could compare with *this* day.

He hoped nothing ever would again.

It should have been a day like any other—better, since he had another pair of special guests to supervise. They meant more work, but handling the new arrivals was considered a prestigious job, essential both to national security and to the island state's economy. Few officers were privileged to deal with one such visitor, and Ahriman Boulard had two.

And that, as Shakespeare once suggested, was the rub.

Boulard had known the man who called himself Charles Stevens was a wanted fugitive. *All* special visitors were hunted men, so that didn't set him apart. Unlike the others, though, the blond American had somehow brought his troubles with him to Victoria. The men who hunted him were here right now, and they were raising hell throughout the Seychelles capital.

Because Boulard had been entrusted with the newest visitors, assigned to get them settled in their new lives, he was also deemed responsible for any problems that arose concerning them. It wasn't strictly fair, but that was life. Boulard wouldn't improve his situation by complaining to the brass, especially since he had already been ordered by his colonel, speaking for the officers above him, to resolve the problem without delay. It would have been most gratifying if he could have carried out that order to the letter, but unfortunately he was stalled.

Boulard had never trained as a detective. He knew nothing of investigative methods, other than the basic job of asking questions. To assist him, he had drafted three plainclothes policemen, but their efforts so far had been fruitless. As he understood police work, most of it involved collecting information from informers on the street and using what they learned to pin an unsolved crime on some specific individual. In this case, such techniques were worthless, since the men he sought had no roots in the community, no contacts to exploit.

Or did they?

Boulard was certain of two things: the men who hunted Stevens had to be new arrivals in the Seychelles, and they had to have come unarmed. Since they were clearly armed with military weapons now, that meant they had acquired the hardware sometime after they arrived, most likely in Victoria. And that in turn told Boulard that a bargain had been struck with one or more of the illicit weapons dealers who were operating in the city. All of them were known to the police; they all paid hefty bribes to stay in business, and occasionally served the state police as stool pigeons when weapons they had sold for self-defense were unaccountably employed in violent crimes.

Until that afternoon, such incidents were few and far between, the dealers trading mostly with the upper class and their employees—bodyguards, chauffeurs, house staff, perhaps some operators in the drug trade. There had never been a spate of homicides like this in all the history of the republic.

While police ran down their list of weapons dealers, Boulard sat in his car and studied the remains of what had been a warehouse owned by Anton Mayer. In fact, Mayer's jet black BMW was still parked beside the ruins of the warehouse, showing giant blisters on its paint, where heat from the explosion and resulting fire had done its work.

As for the owner, his remains and those of a presumed employee were already at the crowded morgue, awaiting autopsy. It would require the use of dental charts to finally decide which man was which, since both were badly charred. A witness to the murders said that both men had been shot before the fire broke out, so there was mercy in the universe, at least.

The witness was a slender man with oily hair combed straight back from his pointed ferret face. He smiled too much, considering the poor state of his teeth, and struggled to ingratiate himself with everyone he met. Boulard suspected that he could turn vicious when he dealt with others smaller and weaker than himself. It would have pleased Boulard to kick his teeth in, but instead he gave the man five hundred rupees, pulling back before the witness had a chance to shake his hand.

The man had provided a description of the gunman who shot Anton Mayer and his warehouse foreman. It was vague—tall, dark, perhaps American—but still, it was their first real information since the killings had begun. Boulard knew this attack was linked with those before it, since the man had left another of his flyers with the witness, giving him instructions that the paper should be handed to police.

Boulard unfolded it, skimmed the familiar contents and the photograph of Stevens, staring at the last line for a moment: "Give him up." Whoever was responsible for the attacks clearly meant that message for the Seychelles authorities. Who else could "give up" one of the protected individuals whom Boulard was assigned to chaperon?

He wondered for a moment if the hunters also sought Afif Rahman. No mention had been made of him so far, but he was obviously linked to Stevens. It was very curious, and Boulard despised unanswered questions, unsolved mysteries. He had already spoken to Stevens in the nature of a friendly warning.

Now, he thought, it was past time for him to call upon the Palestinian and find out if Rahman could help identify the gunmen Boulard would have to find and kill before it was too late.

THE PHONE CALL WAS a gamble. Bolan risked a trace, not knowing whether he could even reach an individual with pull enough to do the job, but Hal Brognola had managed to provide him with a name and number, and he couldn't let it go to waste. Caller ID wouldn't lock on a mobile telephone, and since the first call would be bound to take them by surprise, they shouldn't have triangulation gear in place, assuming it existed in the Seychelles.

To play it extrasafe, he tapped out the number while he was driving, waited through four rings until a sleepy-sounding voice responded, "Ministry of Immigration."

"Let me talk to Ahriman Boulard," Bolan said.

"Major Boulard is not available just now. If you could leave a—"

"Patch me through to his location *now*. I have important information on the recent shootings, and he won't be happy if we can't connect."

"A moment, please."

Major Boulard? So now the Seychelles military was involved in covering for foreign fugitives. It came as no surprise to Bolan, but he felt a certain disappointment, as he always did when men in uniform went bad.

It crossed his mind that the delay in his connection might be someone's bright idea for tracing back the call, but he dismissed it as a danger. With a mobile telephone or radio, triangulation would require at least two spotters in the field, and preferably three, outfitted with the proper gear. Assuming that the Seychelles government possessed that capability, the trackers would have needed to anticipate his call and hit the streets before he dialed in order to catch Bolan in their web.

And yet, if the delay dragged on too long...

"Hold for the major, please." The voice in Bolan's ear didn't sound sleepy anymore.

"Yes, who am I speaking to?"

"Names aren't important," Bolan said. "I understand you've had some trouble lately."

"Trouble, yes," the major replied, "but we are confident that it will be resolved."

"I wouldn't be so sure if I were you."

"If you have information—"

"Tell you what," Bolan said, interrupting him. "I can make sure your problems go away. Of course, I'll need a little something in return."

"Are you admitting knowledge of—"

"Chris Stone. Give him up, and all your problems go away. It's guaranteed."

"I do not recognize the name," Boulard replied.

There was at least a fifty-fifty chance that much was

true. "I don't care what you call him," Bolan said. "You've seen the photographs by now. If you don't know the man yourself, I'm betting you can find someone who does."

"Assuming this were true, you understand that I have certain duties to perform."

"I don't have time for legalistic crap," the Executioner stated. "You want your city back the way it was this morning, nice and peaceful, nothing interfering with the tourist trade. I want Chris Stone...and one more thing."

"Which is?"

As long as he was gambling, Bolan thought, it couldn't hurt to go for broke. "His contact," Bolan said. "The other man. I doubt if they arrived together, but his side-kick won't be far away. In fact, I wouldn't be surprised if he was picking up Stone's tab for the vacation."

There was no immediate denial from Boulard, which told the Executioner that he was on the money. Someone, almost certainly Stone's sponsor, had bailed out of the United States around the same time Stone evacuated, and both men had run to the Seychelles. He guessed that Stone's control had laid the plans and paid the bill, perhaps as some kind of insurance, just in case the stateside deal went sour. Stone, for his part, was a disillusioned soldier who had spent a lifetime chasing foreign wars. It made no sense that he would reach out to the Paul Revere Militia and align himself with their demented cause, unless someone was paying him—and paying handsomely—to take the risk.

"If there was such a man," Boulard replied, "it would not be a simple thing to trick him."

"That's your problem," Bolan said, fresh out of sympathy. "You want your peaceful city back, you know my price. I'll be in touch."

He severed the connection and left Boulard to curse a buzzing dial tone. Bolan hadn't counted on immediate agreement; that kind of surrender was too much to hope for. First, Boulard would have to think about it, as he was right now. Then he would have to run the notion past his boss—a colonel, maybe someone even farther up the ladder of command. That kind of scheming always took some time, but there was no reason for the Executioner to stand idle while the issue was debated. He had targets still untouched, and every blow he struck would add new force, new urgency, to his demands.

AFIF RAHMAN WASN'T surprised when Ahriman Boulard knocked at his door. Dusk was approaching, and the city lights were coming on outside, inviting Rahman to explore Victoria, but something told him that the major hadn't come to take him sight-seeing.

"We have a problem," Boulard said, when he had closed the stout, self-locking door behind him.

"Oh?" Rahman took pride in coping with adversity as a professional, without emotional displays. Among the *fedayeen* of Hezbollah, he had a well-earned reputation for dispassionate, remorseless violence.

"There have been shootings in the city."

"I have been watching them on television," Rahman said, nodding in the direction of the twenty-six-inch monitor in the corner. "What has this to do with me?"

"At every shooting scene, police found one of these." Boulard withdrew a folded piece of paper from his pocket, passed it to Rahman and waited while the Arab scanned its contents. If he hoped for an emotional reaction, he was ultimately disappointed.

"Yes, I see." Rahman met Boulard's eyes again and gave the paper back. "It would appear to me, however, that you should be warning Mr. Stevens...or should I say Stone?"

"I have advised him of the situation," Boulard said. "But it affects you, too."

"I don't see how." The major would read nothing in the man's eyes.

"One of the men responsible for these attacks has telephoned me," Boulard said. "He promises an end to bloodshed if I give him Mr. Stone."

"In that case—"

"And," the major went on, interrupting him, "he wants you, also."

Rahman blinked at that. Where any other man may well have started cursing or recoiled in shock, he had enough control to limit his reaction. One quick blink.

"There must be some mistake," he said.

"Unfortunately, no," Boulard replied. "This man, whoever he may be, told *me* that Mr. Stone—may we agree that is his name?—would have a traveling companion. Furthermore, he guessed, or knew, that this companion would have paid the entry fee for Mr. Stone. There's no mistake."

"I take it that he did not know my name?" Rahman inquired. "There are no flyers with my photograph?"

"Not yet," the major said.

"In that case, I'm afraid I still don't see—"

"There were conditions relevant to your admission," the major said. "You recall them, I believe?"

"Of course." Rahman allowed the barest hint of irritation to show through his calm exterior. This peasant was annoying him. He didn't like the direction their conversation had taken.

"To be clear," Boulard went on, "it was agreed that

there would be no criminal activity associated with your stay in the Republic of Seychelles.''

"There has been none."

"On that point, I must disagree. We now have six men dead, another badly wounded and a warehouse full of costly merchandise destroyed. One of the dead was, like yourself, a special visitor to the republic. Protests have been filed. There is a feeling of...dissatisfaction, shall we say?"

"I'm not responsible for how your clients feel about the service you provide," Rahman replied. "You charge a fee—no small one, I might add—and guarantee security to those who pay. Security not only from indictments, extradition, but from any other form of jeopardy. The present circumstance is more extreme than diplomatic protests, I admit, but there is no real difference in the principle. If you are threatening—"

"I make no threats. I simply thought that you should be aware of what is happening, and what may happen if the situation cannot be resolved."

"That still sounds like an ultimatum, Major."

Boulard was frowning. "I have taken the precaution of assigning guards to you and Mr. Stone," he said. "They will remain in the hotel while you are here and will escort you anywhere you need to go. For safety's sake, of course, it would be best if you did not go out unnecessarily."

"Am I to be confined at house arrest? Is that the service that a million dollars buys in the Republic of Seychelles?"

"By no means," the major said, stiffening. "I simply made a logical suggestion, with your safety foremost in my mind."

"In that case, I appreciate the thought...and the assignment of your soldiers. I assume they will not be in uniform?"

"Plainclothes," Boulard replied. "The last thing we desire is to draw more attention."

"Excellent. In that case, if we're finished...?"

"For the moment, sir. Goodbye."

Alone once more, Rahman relaxed enough to frown. He had no doubt that Boulard's watchdogs were under orders to contain his movements if they could. Failing that, could they protect him from the man or men who had been shooting up Victoria the past few hours? As a last resort, would they attempt to give him up, along with Stone, in order to resolve the problem?

Rahman didn't intend to make it easy for them if there was betrayal in the wind. Already armed, he would defend himself with every means at his disposal, but he hoped it wouldn't come to that. In fact, he was already looking for a way to save himself, eliminate the danger. It was possible that some kind of agreement could be reached between himself and those who hunted him. If they were presently more interested in Stone, perhaps...

In fact, Rahman decided, that might solve two problems simultaneously. If Chris Stone was taken out by the anonymous pursuers, it would be a relatively simple task for Hezbollah to reach out and reclaim the money Stone had already been paid. There would be no objection from a dead man, no retaliation from beyond the grave.

The more he thought about it in that light, the more Rahman approved of the idea. But it would take some planning yet. He couldn't rush, risk bungling it, for there would be no second chance. He didn't care for the possibility of Chris Stone stalking *him* when he was already at risk.

Be cautious, then, but get it done. And soon.

Rahman sat down to strip and clean his weapons prior to leaving the hotel. He had some errands that had waited long enough. The news from Boulard made them more urgent than before. His bodyguards could either tag along or try to stop him, but he hoped they could avoid unpleasantness for yet a little while.

Until his own trap was prepared and ready to be sprung.

11

Stone had agreed to meet Afif Rahman again, but he insisted that the meeting should be held on neutral ground. Which was to say in public, where the Arab would have less chance of arranging for an ambush to eliminate his "friend."

Things had been getting too damn weird for Stone the past few hours. It unnerved him that he was already being hunted here, in the Republic of Seychelles, when he had taken pains to hide his tracks. Goddamn technology these days, he thought...or had somebody sold him out? If so, there was a short list of prospective traitors he would have to deal with when the time was right.

No one in the militia—hell, nobody in the States—had known where he was going when he split from Florida, except Rahman. If Stone applied himself, he could imagine several reasons why the Arab might decide to stab him in the back, not least of them the urge to keep from paying Stone his last installment on the sum they had contracted eighteen months before. Fanatics like Hezbollah commandos talked a lot about their holy mission, giving up their souls to God in a great jihad, but they would also pinch a penny until it screamed. Especially these days, when the wellspring of support from Russia had dried up, and dickheads like Khaddafi and Saddam Hussein had grown more circumspect about expenditures.

Still, money wouldn't be the only reason if Rahman had sold him out. Stone was the one man who could link Hezbollah to crimes committed by the Paul Revere Militia and the ASA back home. There was a chance, however minimal, that he would spill the beans to save himself if he was taken into custody. Rahman was one of those who only trusted natives of his own homeland, and only then if they had sworn a blood oath to the cause. He had regarded Chris Stone with a thinly veiled contempt since they first met, a mercenary who chose sides in any given conflict based upon that side's ability to pay in cash.

Of course, Rahman wasn't Stone's only candidate for traitor of the month. It was entirely possible that someone there in the Seychelles had dropped a quarter, although he found the likelihood remote. Tourism was the lifeblood of the island, with a sideline in providing sanctuary for assorted fugitives, and both trades would be jeopardized by gunplay in the streets. There was an outside chance that someone like his chaperon, Ahriman Boulard, would sell him out, expecting Stone to be arrested peacefully, without a fuss, only to have the whole thing blow up in his face. But why?

On balance, Stone would put his money on Rahman, but he couldn't accuse the Arab openly. Not yet. A phone check with his bank informed Stone that the last deposit due under his contract hadn't been received. It never would be if he caused a scene with his employer now, much less if he should lose his cool and kill Rahman outright. The old saw said that haste made waste, and Stone wasn't prepared to waste the magic goose before he had those golden eggs in hand.

But he would be prepared when they sat down together, yes indeed. He had retrieved his mini-Uzi from the dealer, no small chore with the official shadows forced upon him by his chaperon, Boulard. Stone didn't know if they were hip to what he had acquired or not, but they made no attempt to confiscate the piece, and that was fine. When he went out to meet Rahman the second time that day, he wore the mini-Uzi in a makeshift sling beneath his right arm, while the Browning pistols were nestled in his belt. It was a good thing that he wouldn't be called upon to pass through any metal detectors, Stone thought. If he was cornered, though, he would be able to defend himself with an impressive fireworks show.

In other circumstances, Stone imagined that he might have liked Victoria. Someplace to visit, anyway, although he wouldn't want to live there. When a man was being hunted, though, all cities were the same: a maze of streets and alleys that had to be navigated with absolute precision; windows that could hide a hundred snipers in a given block; vehicles passing by that could erupt in automatic-weapons fire at any moment. Stone had played the game from both sides in his time, and when it came to stalking, he could guarantee that it was more enjoyable to give than to receive.

At least his bodyguards didn't insist on walking with him, as if they were all the best of friends. They hung back far enough to let Stone have some room, but they were never out of sight—or out of pistol shot. At first, he had suspected that they might be shooters sent to kill him under cover of "protection," but there had been ample opportunity for them to make a move by now. He could relax a little with the two men trailing him, as if he had six eyes instead of two. Presumably they were professionals and could be helpful when it came to spotting traps. Hell, if the shooting started, one of them might even stop a bullet meant for Stone.

He left the Hotel Marcellais two hours early for his

meeting, skipped the taxicab and walked four blocks to reach the public square that had been chosen for his meeting with Rahman. He walked around the square, two laps to memorize the layout, checking it for any indications of an ambush in the making, then retired to a little hole-in-the-wall restaurant nearby, where he took a window seat and ordered curried chicken. Stone's two shadows couldn't find an open table and were forced to wait outside.

Too bad.

He took his time, enjoyed the meal and washed it down with coffee. He would have much preferred some wine, or even beer. He needed steady hands, though, for the night ahead, in case Rahman had some trick up his sleeve and Stone was forced to shoot his way out of the meeting.

If that happened, he would learn which side his bodyguards were really on. And if they let him down, well, everybody was expendable. So what?

IT WAS A BAD SIGN, Boulard decided, when the colonel didn't ask him to sit down. Most of their meetings were remarkably informal—or as much as they could be, at least, within the general framework of prevailing military discipline. This time, however, Colonel Etan Roux didn't stand when Boulard entered his office, nor did he direct the major to either of the stylish chairs that faced his desk.

Bad news, and no mistake.

"What progress have you made toward the solution of our problem?" Roux inquired without preliminary salutations.

"Sir, I have discussed the matter with both visitors, and have assigned two guards to watch each man. Investigation is continuing into the several incidents, so far without result."

"Without result," the colonel echoed him. "That is not what I wish to hear."

"No, sir." Of course it wasn't what the colonel wished to hear, but it was still the truth. Boulard could have arrested suspects on the flimsiest of evidence, perhaps even succeeded in convicting one or more of them if he had handled it correctly, but the threat would still remain.

"You understand the gravity of this disturbance?" the colonel asked.

"Yes, sir."

Roux proceeded to explain, as if Boulard had never answered him. "These incidents are perilous to the Seychelles economy, Major. Not only are our special visitors alarmed, with others no doubt thinking twice about investing here, but violence in the streets is also bad for tourism. You understand all this?"

"Yes, sir." An imbecile could understand it. What Boulard could *not* do was allow himself to take offense at anything the colonel said, no matter how insulting it might be. He had his job and pension to consider, after all.

"In that case, can you tell me what steps you have taken to resolve the problem, other than providing bodyguards for these two individuals?"

"Yes, sir." It felt as if his larynx was constricting. He could barely force the words out. It was all Boulard could do to keep from tugging at his tie and gasping like a stranded fish.

"We are collaborating with police," he said, "to find and interview potential suspects. We assume the man or men responsible for these attacks is an American—a foreigner, at least."

"Brilliant detective work," the colonel fairly sneered.

"With that in mind," Boulard went on, "we are reviewing passport records for the past two days, assuming that the man or men we seek has only just arrived in the republic.''

''Why?''

Boulard assumed that Roux had to know the answer. He was being tested, and he dared not fail. ''Because the two guests singled out, Rahman and Stone, have only just arrived themselves. Their flights were booked mere hours in advance. It seems unlikely that the men who hunt them could have known they would be coming here beforehand.''

''This Rahman, the Arab,'' Roux put in, ''has still not been identified in any of the warning notices recovered from the crime scenes?''

''No, sir.''

''With that in mind, Major, what leads you to believe that he needs bodyguards? Why should we think he faces any risk at all?''

''Because, sir, it was he who paid the entry fee for Mr. Stone,'' Boulard replied. ''We know they are associated. That much is established fact. As for the details, well, we make a point of not inquiring, as you know. It seemed imperative, however, to protect both men if they are to remain with us.''

The colonel cocked an eyebrow, frowning. ''Has either one of them expressed a wish to leave?''

''No, sir. That is, not yet.''

''A pity. It would help us very much, I think, if one or both of them should choose to go elsewhere.''

''Agreed, sir, but there is a risk in asking them to go. Before long, I suspect, the word would circulate among prospective special visitors. Those with concerns about security would certainly look elsewhere in the future.''

"I am not suggesting that these men be asked to leave. That choice would have to be their own, made voluntarily."

"Yes, sir. I understand."

"And if a visitor decides to leave entirely of his own accord, while we are doing everything within our power to protect him, he could not expect a refund of his entry fee."

"It would establish a disturbing precedent, sir. I agree."

Roux's grimace told Boulard that he couldn't have cared less whether his subordinate agreed with him. "Of course," the colonel said, "ideally we should hope to find the men responsible for these attacks and punish them. If they turn out to be Americans, a protest could be filed with the United Nations, citing violation of our national integrity."

Boulard was almost forced to smile at that, considering the ill repute his homeland had already gained by offering protection to a whole rogue's gallery of fugitives from justice. As it was, he bit his lip and said nothing, waiting for the colonel to proceed.

"These hypothetical Americans," Roux said at last, "how would you deal with them?"

"Sir, I would treat them just like any other criminal. They must be held for trial. Of course, we know that they are armed and dangerous. If they resist arrest..." He let the statement trail away, unfinished. Colonel Roux would understand what he was getting at. There was no need to spell it out.

"With such men," Roux remarked, "I would assume that armed resistance is anticipated."

"The police have been advised, sir. None of them are

anxious to be shot. They have been authorized to use all necessary force."

"And if they fail, you will have people of your own on hand to help them?"

"Yes, sir. Since the minister of tourism was kind enough to speak with the police commissioner, our men have been invited to participate directly in the search."

"Directly, but not obviously," Roux suggested.

"No, sir. Never that."

"And you expect results." It was a statement, not a question. Boulard could feel the colonel's dark eyes boring into him like drill bits.

"Yes, sir. I am confident that we will find and neutralize the men responsible for these outrageous crimes."

The colonel smiled and said, "For your sake, Major, I sincerely hope you are correct."

"Yes, sir."

There was no more to say. Boulard had been dismissed, and he was glad to leave the colonel's presence. He had too much work to do to waste more time in idle conversation, listening to threats.

He dared not fail this time, because his own life now depended on the outcome of the hunt.

Boulard dismissed the very notion of defeat. He knew the city and its people, those on both sides of the law. With the cooperation of police, he would not, *could* not, fail.

Not if he wanted to maintain his rank and privileges.

Not if he hoped to stay alive.

AFIF RAHMAN'S ADVANCE man in Victoria was a young Palestinian, Muhammad Alhazred, who had been with Hezbollah five years, since he had turned fifteen. Before that, he had volunteered his services as an errand boy, delivering messages, and never missed a chance to stone Israeli soldiers in a riot. Since enlisting as a full-fledged member of the *fedayeen*, Alhazred had proved himself reliable, a killer who felt nothing for his victims, caring only for the cause. He would do anything to protect his fellow warriors and destroy the Zionist invaders of his great ancestral homeland.

Now he sat and listened while Rahman explained what they had to do together to prevent the cause from being jeopardized by one who had been hired to serve God. Alhazred despised all mercenaries on principle, and he reserved a special contempt for American soldiers of fortune, those hypocrites who spoke about the land of opportunity while hiring out their guns to tin-pot dictators around the world. He hadn't met the blond American named Stone—had never heard his name before that afternoon, in fact—but now Alhazred hoped that he would be allowed to kill the man. He said as much, and watched Rahman consider it before he frowned and shook his head.

"Not yet. It may come to that if we can find no other method to dispose of him, but I prefer another way if we can make it work."

"As you command," Alhazred replied. His disappointment wasn't audible, nor did it surface in his eyes.

"It would be best for all concerned," Rahman continued, "if the men who seek our friend so diligently should, in fact, discover where he is."

Alhazred was smart enough to see the wisdom in that plan. There was a chance that Hezbollah might need to use more mercenaries in the future, and it would be difficult for them if they were known to kill off their employees, rather than fulfilling every detail of their contracts. On the other hand, if someone else should kill the blond American, well, that would simply be bad luck. A

mercenary soldier took his chances in the world, and most
of them had enemies who wouldn't shrink from murder.

"I am still not certain how such an event may be ar-
ranged," Rahman went on. It seemed to his companion
that the older man was talking to himself. "There has to
be a way, and yet..."

"Would the authorities cooperate?" Alhazred asked.

Rahman considered it. "All things are possible, but at
the moment, I suspect the Seychellois would like to see
us both evaporate. To ask their help in such a matter...no.
It is impossible. They would find some way to betray us
in the end."

"This man, the major," Alhazred said. "If he has
threatened you, I can chastise him for his insolence."

Rahman couldn't resist a smile at that. "Your loyalty
is appreciated," he replied, "but at the moment, I prefer
to cultivate a good relationship with the authorities. Major
Boulard can wait until we are prepared to leave. When
that time comes, you may chastise him with my
blessing."

"Thank you." Alhazred was smiling, too.

"As for our main problem, we cannot offer up Stone
to his enemies until we find out who they are and how to
get in touch with them."

"You said that Stone named one of them," the young
man said.

"Indeed. But even he believes the name—Belasko, I
believe it was—to be a cover. His description of the man
could fit half of the tourists in Victoria, assuming that the
same man even came to the Seychelles."

"And this American, the nameless one, does not know
you?"

"Nothing suggests it. Only Stone and his American associates have been attacked before today. If this Belasko

or his people knew that I was here, that I employed the man they seek, there should have been some effort to destroy me, also."

"It's too bad," Alhazred said.

"What is?"

The younger man shrugged. "If you were known to those men hunting Stone, if they were watching you, then it would be a simple thing to lead them by the nose until they found him."

"True enough," Rahman replied, "but they might then decide to murder me instead. And how could I lead them to Stone unless I placed myself in the same trap?"

"You would not have to lead them physically," Alhazred answered. "If they tapped your telephone, for instance, you could set a meeting with this mercenary, tell him where to go and have the hunters there ahead of him."

"It is a good idea," Rahman allowed. "Unfortunately I do not believe the telephones are tapped—by the Americans, at any rate."

"We could pretend they are," the young man said.

"Explain."

"You have a meeting scheduled with the mercenary, yes?" Alhazred didn't wait for the older man to nod before continuing. "When he arrives, I could be waiting for him. Everyone already knows that he is being hunted through the city. If he should be killed while you are with him, and you narrowly escape, no blame could be attached to you. The Seychelles authorities would keep on looking for the men who staged these other raids, and the Americans, in turn, would have their dead man. If they do not know your name already, there is every chance that they would not pursue the matter further."

"You surprise me," Rahman said. "It is a cunning plan. I like it."

Sitting on the sofa, slender hands clasped in his lap, Muhammad Alhazred could feel the grin light up his face from ear to ear.

GAETAN MALLEVILLE HAD served eleven years as a policeman in Victoria before he was dismissed on charges of corruption. He hadn't been prosecuted, but dismissal had relieved him of his pension and had left him virtually unemployable in any decent job. The latter part of it was no great problem, since Malleville wasn't known to his enemies or friends as a particularly decent man. He mourned the pension, though, because he loved the thought of being paid to do nothing.

The whole thing with his job had been a farce, as Malleville saw it. He had been no more corrupt that any other lawman in Victoria—at least, no more than any of the ones he hung around with, plotting ways to steal. If there were honest cops around, they didn't trouble Malleville, and he didn't take the time to learn their names. He was too busy doubling, then tripling his official salary in bribes from sundry miscreants, including pimps, drug dealers, thieves and independent prostitutes who reckoned they could stay in business longer if their faces were intact.

If it had only been the bribes, Malleville was confident that he wouldn't have been dismissed. Instead, he blamed the whole thing on a little weasel of a pimp named Jules Roget. The bastard had been holding out on Malleville, underreporting what he earned each week in order to reduce the bribes he paid. When Malleville found out about his treachery, it was essential that Roget be chastised publicly, as an example to his kind.

Still, he never meant to kill the man. He had been working on Roget, with knuckle-dusters and his steel-toed boots, when some deranged impulse made Roget strike back in his own defense. It was a glancing blow, no force behind it, and it barely made Malleville's lip bleed, but he had gone berserk from the affront, ripping into Roget with a madman's strength until he realized that he had gone too far. Because there had been witnesses, including five or six French tourists passing by the alleyway in broad daylight, with Malleville wearing full uniform, there had been no chance for him to escape the special hearing that eventually left him unemployed.

But not for long.

A bare two months had passed before his government, the one he used to serve, announced its plan to welcome fugitives from foreign lands if they could pay the price for sanctuary in the Seychelles. A short time later, Gaetan Malleville had been approached by one of his old cronies on the force, who asked if he would like to share in the rewards that the new program was expected to produce.

It seemed that certain members of the ruling party had grown squeamish in the face of public criticism aimed at their new money-making scheme. They wouldn't drop the plan, but neither did they care for the idea of regular policemen guarding foreign criminals as if they were respected diplomats assigned to work in the Seychelles. Instead, it was suggested that "someone" should organize a small, efficient paramilitary force to deal with the security concerns of special visitors. Members of the detachment would be used as bodyguards—or in the worst scenario, as "cleaners," to dispose of any interlopers who attempted to subvert the government's legitimate activities. In that way, there would be no public trials, no ongoing embarrassment.

And it had been what the Americans would call a piece of cake, so far, until that very afternoon. Now all Victoria was up in arms about a series of attacks on random targets, seemingly designed to force delivery of one special visitor into the hands of those responsible for the bloodshed. Two new arrivals were supposedly involved, at risk, and Malleville had given each of them two bodyguards, around the clock. Now Major Ahriman Boulard had called him on the telephone to say it wasn't good enough.

"We need to find the men responsible for these outrages," Boulard said, the tension in his voice as palpable as if he had a hacking cough. "*You* need to find them."

"It will not be easy," Malleville replied. "We have a vague description of one man, who may or may not be involved in the attacks. I can't stop every stranger on the island and demand to know if he's been killing people. I don't have the manpower, for one thing."

"You have other sources, though," Boulard pressed on. "Arms dealers and the like. You *could* go after them."

"But the police know who they are as well as I," Malleville replied. "Why aren't they asking?"

"They are handling the regular investigation," Boulard said. "As for the rest of it, this is the very kind of work your unit was established for. Need I remind you of the generous amount you have been paid?"

Malleville was in no mood for smug reminders, or for ultimatums, if it came to that. "I know my job," he said, "and I will do it. But it will not be accomplished quickly. You should be prepared for some delay, the possibility of more attacks while we are waiting for the necessary information to be found."

"The longer we delay," Boulard said, "the greater likelihood we have of being unemployed...or worse."

Malleville had already been unemployed. It held no terrors for him, since he knew a thousand ways to earn his daily bread. He was concerned about "or worse," however. There were many ways for men to suffer, beyond cutting off a paycheck. You could always cut off other things.

"I'll do my best," he said. "No promises."

"Then I will promise you," Boulard came back at him, "that if you cannot solve this problem, you are useless. Do you understand? You serve no purpose whatsoever."

There it was.

"I'm working on it," he responded peevishly. "If I can find these men, how do you want them?"

"I *don't* want them. Use your imagination. Make the bastards go away."

12

No more Mr. Nice Guy. Bolan was taking off the gloves, and he had a list of targets waiting for him, scattered all over Victoria.

He had decided to postpone his second chat with Ahriman Boulard until he rattled the major's cage some more. Bolan was pushing it, he realized, demanding both Chris Stone and his anonymous associate, seeking a government betrayal of two clients for the price of one, but it was worth a shot. He knew there was a sponsor, and while he wasn't totally convinced the sponsor would have turned up in Victoria along with Stone, Major Boulard's reaction had confirmed the hunch. It was a relatively simple matter now of turning up the heat until Boulard and company couldn't afford to keep their bargain with the mercenary and his master.

Simple, right. Like plunging headfirst down an old, abandoned well.

The list of names and addresses was written down, but Bolan also had it memorized. He ran it through his mind while studying a street map of Victoria, and lined up half a dozen strikes that would, if luck was with him, carry him across the city, moving west to east. If he was nailed somewhere along the way, it would make no great difference which direction he was moving or what names were on his list of targets.

Dead was dead, and that applied to executioners as well as to their prey.

Full darkness had descended on the city, and there was some kind of party going on when Bolan reached the first stop on his list. He thought of giving it a pass, but then a second look at the expensive cars outside the chic suburban home convinced him he should stick around. The party-goers were civilians, granted, and as innocent as anyone could be who lived in a society that harbored felons, rubbing shoulders with outcast scum of other nations, he didn't mean to kill them. Shake them up a little, perhaps, and send the shock waves rippling back to those in charge of fugitive protection.

That would do just fine.

He came in through the back, avoiding the chauffeurs out front. Some of them might be armed, doubling as bodyguards, and while it wouldn't faze him to eliminate some button men while he was at it, Bolan had his heart set on a different kind of razzle-dazzle for this social outing. He was carrying the MP-5 K submachine gun, the Beretta and a couple of grenades, but hoped he could get away with sound and fury rather than an epic body count.

The fence was nothing, and he scaled it in two seconds flat. Nobody seemed to notice as he came in at them from the darkness, well beyond the floodlights covering the patio and pool, the whole rear of the house. No one was swimming at the moment, though a number of attractive women had stripped down to skimpy bathing suits, and Bolan saw his chance to open with a bang.

He palmed one of the Russian frag grenades, released the safety pin and tossed the bomb underhand into the deep end of the swimming pool. It sank almost completely to the bottom prior to detonating, and the ice blue water managed to contain the shrapnel, even as a geyser spouted skyward with a muffled roar.

Some of the women started to scream, while the men were mostly startled into silence. One or two of them recovered more quickly than the others, laughing at what they perceived as a bizarre display of fireworks. Bolan changed their minds when he began to unload with the SMG, first taking out the floodlights with a series of precision bursts, then spraying the remainder of a magazine above the heads of the frightened guests as they began a stampede back into the house.

The Executioner began to reload as he followed them inside. With any luck at all, he still might get to huddle with his host—a multimillionaire stock swindler from Canada.

IT WAS FULL DARK when Stone left the café and started walking toward the meeting place he had selected for his sit-down with Afif Rahman. Of course, they might not actually *sit down*. In fact, the time that he had killed already, watching out for traps around the public square, had left Stone nervous, jumpy in a way that he couldn't recall since he had come out on the clean side of his first few combat missions in the Special Forces.

The square had tourists in it even now, when most of the surrounding shops were closed or on the verge of shutting down. They were sightseers, mostly, men and women walking hand in hand, or arm in arm if they were older. There were statues in the square. Stone didn't know or care exactly what they were supposed to represent, but he moved in that direction, drifting toward the central piece. A guidebook could have told him who or what the statue was, but Stone had zero interest in the subject. He was watching for Afif Rahman and anyone the Arab may have brought along with him to shift the odds.

Behind him, Stone's two uninvited bodyguards were hanging back, as they had done since he bailed out of the hotel. No socializing on their part, and it was just as well, since Stone had nothing that he cared to share with rent-a-cops. Rahman, when he appeared, was trailing two more plainclothesmen in his wake, and while the sight of them should logically have put Stone's mind at ease, he couldn't bring himself to fully trust the Arab.

Rahman was smiling as the gap between them closed, but Stone had the impression that the smile was forced, unnatural. Perhaps, he thought, it was because the Arab normally refrained from smiling altogether, making any crack in the facade appear suspicious and bizarre.

Perhaps.

"You brought your shadows," Rahman commented, when they were close enough for shaking hands.

"I didn't have much choice," Stone said.

"I, also. Shall we walk?"

"Suits me."

"I have been giving thought," Rahman went on, "to our peculiar problem."

"So?"

"I think—"

The bullet passed within an inch or less of Stone's right ear, so close that he could feel it sizzle through the air. He recognized that feeling, ducked his head and was half-way to the deck before he heard the crack of gunfire somewhere on his right, and to the rear.

He landed on his shoulder, rolled and came up kneeling, with the mini-Uzi in his hand. It would do little good against a sniper firing from a distance, but it made him feel better, regardless. And besides, if there was one shooter, there might be—

"You!"

Rahman was staring at him from six or seven feet away, and the expression on his face was one of irritation rather than surprise. That quickly, in the time it took his pounding heart to pump one spurt of blood and suck another in, Stone knew the Arab had indeed prepared a lethal trap for him. The merc didn't know the triggerman; such minor details were irrelevant in any case. He knew only that he had to kill Rahman before the sniper got him zeroed in.

He braced the mini-Uzi in a two-handed grip, and he was lining up the shot when something struck the little SMG and knocked it spinning from his hands. More bullets swarmed around him, one of them a searing brand across his side, and Stone recoiled, lunged through a backward somersault and came up in the shadow of the statue, briefly hidden from the man who sought to take his life.

Rahman was running for it back across the plaza, knees and elbows pumping as he sprinted for his life. Stone drew one of the Browning semiautos and thumbed off the safety, but when he tried to aim, he found his hands were trembling, maybe still vibrating from the bullet's impact with his weapon. Stone fired anyway, two quick ones in the darkness, but he missed Rahman both times.

Their four bodyguards had weapons drawn, and had begun to return fire in the direction of a rooftop sniper's nest across the way. Unfortunately for the grim quartet, they carried only handguns, while the sniper had some kind of semiautomatic rifle. His aim was getting better, cutting down first one of Stone's assigned protectors, then one of Rahman's.

Stone didn't wait around to see the others die. He was already off and running, trying desperately to keep the statue at his back, between the sniper and himself. It seemed to take forever, covering the forty yards or so to shelter. Only when he found himself well down a narrow, darkened side street did the mercenary let himself relax.

And start to think about revenge.

GAETAN MALLEVILLE HAD made up his mind to begin with weapons dealers in Victoria. It was the best, most logical approach, since any strangers in the Seychelles would find it very difficult to smuggle in firearms, and relatively simple—if expensive—to acquire them after they had passed through customs, free and clear. He had a list of dealers, half a dozen names, that he would check before he got around to searching yachts in the marina, raiding hotel rooms and initiating other, more disruptive tactics.

The first name on his list was Maurice Betancourt. The man sold sporting goods to tourists, everything from swimsuits, tanning lotion and sunglasses to high-priced scuba gear and "action" clothes designed in Paris. On the side, he dealt in guns and ammunition.

Betancourt was only one of several outlaw firearms dealers in the Seychelles capital, and Malleville had no good reason to believe he had done business with the terrorists who had been shooting up the town. In fact, no matter what he learned from this initial visit, the security man meant to speak with each and every dealer on his list. If they were innocent, they would experience some brief discomfort, but they would survive. He might even mock up an apology if he was in the mood. If one of them confessed, it would be quite another matter, but he still planned to run the whole list anyway, in case the men he sought had purchased arms from more than one supplier.

Every bit of information he acquired along the way would bring him closer to his prey.

As for Betancourt and his associates, well, they would understand. It was a price of doing business on the wrong side of the law.

The shop was closed when Malleville and his men arrived, but that was no impediment, since Betancourt lived upstairs. They simply hammered on the door and rang the bell until an upstairs window opened up and someone shouted down, "We're closed!"

"You're open," Malleville corrected, stepping back to let the streetlight show his face. "We have important business to discuss, Maurice."

He couldn't hear the dealer cursing, but Malleville had a fair idea of how he had to be feeling. Any summons after dark was normally bad news, and when the message was delivered by a man like Gaetan Malleville, in company with others of his ilk, bad news was frequently the very worst.

He waited, growing more impatient by the moment, until lights went on inside the shop, and he could see Betancourt approaching, buttoning a short-sleeved shirt over his chest. The gun dealer was nearly bald and wore thick glasses that kept sliding halfway down his crooked nose, forcing him to push them back again, a gesture that had graduated to the status of a habit, almost like a nervous tic. The gun dealer unlocked the door, backpedaling as Malleville and his troops barged through, one of them pausing to secure the latch behind them.

"What do you want?"

"That's not a very friendly attitude, Maurice," Malleville replied. "Especially since I've allowed you to remain in business all these years. It would have been so easy, so enjoyable, to shut you down at any time."

"What have I done?"

"That's what *I* want to know, Maurice. You watch the television, I suppose?"

"Yes. I was watching it just now."

"You know about the trouble, then."

"Trouble?"

"The shootings in Victoria, Maurice." Malleville allowed a cutting edge to creep into his voice. "If you insist on acting like an imbecile, I'll treat you like one."

He had barely finished speaking when he lashed out and struck Betancourt across the face, an open-handed slap that sent his glasses flying. The gun dealer was staggered, catching himself before he fell by reaching out to grasp the corner of a glass display case filled with scuba masks and fins in varied colors.

"Please, Gaetan!"

"I don't enjoy this," Malleville informed the dealer, lying through his teeth. "It is a duty I despise, but duty all the same. I am tasked to learn who sold the weapons to these villains. You must tell me anything you know about this matter. If you lie, I will find out and hurt you badly. Do you understand?"

"Gaetan, I—"

Betancourt was silenced by a short jab to the solar plexus, thrown in from his blind side by the hulk on Malleville's left. He doubled over, gasping, speechless, and one of the other men unleashed a roundhouse punch that straightened him again, blood spurting from his nose. This time he didn't catch himself, but rather wound up on the floor, surrounded by his tormentors.

"I asked a simple question," Malleville reminded him. "Now, do you understand, Maurice?"

"Yes."

"Say it."

"Yes, I understand, Gaetan."

"I knew you would. You always were a wise one, eh, Maurice?" His tone had almost lost the edge, but there was steel beneath the velvet of his words. "Now, I propose to ask you certain questions. You will answer honestly, I hope. It would be most unfortunate if we were forced to ask your wife and lovely daughter, would it not?"

"Please, no, Gaetan!"

"You will cooperate?"

"You know I will."

"Stand up, then, and behave yourself. Stop wriggling like a worm."

Betancourt had trouble getting up, and one of Malleville's soldiers had to help him. With his lower face awash in blood, the gun dealer resembled someone who had been caught eating from a pot of fresh strawberry jam. The security man produced a handkerchief and handed it over.

"Your face," he said.

The dealer nodded, dabbing at his nostrils, grimacing in pain at the unwelcome contact. He didn't retrieve his glasses, and without them he was forced to squint at Malleville, as if the other man were standing far away.

"I need to know if any strangers have come calling in the past two days," Malleville said, "for guns. You understand?"

"Yes," the dealer said, and blew a crimson bubble from one nostril. "Yes, Gaetan. I understand."

13

"You were supposed to kill him with the first shot," said Rahman. "How could you miss?"

Alhazred made no excuses. "I have failed," he said, eyes downcast, shoulders slumping as he spoke. "My life is yours."

"I do not need your life," Rahman snapped. "I needed his."

"At least I killed the others." It was the first attempt Alhazred had made to justify himself since he had joined Afif Rahman after the shooting in the public square.

"They were no threat to us," Rahman reminded him. "Two of them were my bodyguards. All four were agents of the Seychelles government."

"I will keep looking," the younger man said. "Stone cannot hide forever. He may possibly be wounded. I can find him and—"

"There is no time to waste," Rahman informed him, interrupting. "I must get out of the city while I can, and you are coming with me, for security."

"As you require. My life is yours."

Rahman had leased a house outside Victoria, not huge, but large enough, with grounds resembling a minijungle, shrubs and trees run riot. He had been planning to stay there, instead of at the Hotel Marcellais, and now he was relieved to have the fallback option readily at hand. Stone didn't know about the house, and while he might be able to acquire that information even as a hunted man, if he decided to come looking for Rahman he would be on the Arab's turf. It was perfect.

"You have everything we need?" Rahman asked his subordinate.

"I have the car, the weapons and your luggage," Alhazred replied. "If there is something else..."

"No. We should leave at once before that fool Boulard comes asking more of his insufferable questions."

Boulard *did* know about the rented house, of course. There was a chance he would show up there, nagging Rahman with his questions, but there was no help for that. If he insisted on more bodyguards, the Palestinian was going to demand a team with proper training, rather than the kind of idiots who had been slaughtered in the plaza. It was a lucky thing indeed, Rahman decided, that the ambush had been his idea. If someone else had been responsible, with "help" like that, Rahman would almost certainly be dead.

Alhazred had the car in gear and rolling, keeping to the smaller, darker streets as much as possible, avoiding traffic when he could. They weren't being followed, but there was a risk, however slight, of being spotted by a government patrol that might be seeking them already, ordered up by Boulard to hold Rahman for questioning.

He considered how he should respond to the inevitable grilling, easily deciding that complete denial was the way to go. The shooting in the plaza was another in the series of attacks that had already stunned Victoria. It was a shame about his bodyguards, but they had done their job after a fashion, buying time for him to get away. Of course, he hadn't waited for Boulard to get in touch. Why should he, when the rented house was waiting for him, and his life was threatened every moment that he lingered in Victoria? The second pair of dead men would reveal that Stone was also in the plaza when the shooting started, but Rahman, in truth, had no idea where the American had gone from there. Perhaps he could describe the shooting as Stone's work, and thereby set the bloodhounds on his trail. If Rahman truly understood the mercenary's mind-set, Stone wouldn't surrender meekly to arrest. He would resist with all the force at his disposal.

Stone gunned down by the authorities, or by Muhammad Alhazred, was still Stone dead, and that was all that mattered to Rahman. As far as he could tell, the mercenary was his only concrete link to what had happened in the States, in Mexico, in the Seychelles. Once the American was gone, the men who hunted him would soon lose interest—or at least run out of targets—and they would give up the chase. A few more weeks of exile, then, and Rahman could rejoin his friends in Hezbollah, renew his war against the Zionists.

He didn't realize that he was smiling grimly, like a death's-head, in the feeble dashboard light.

MAJOR BOULARD WAS sick and tired of corpses. There were four of them this time, and they were all his men—or, rather, they were Gaetan Malleville's. Still, it had been Boulard who called on Malleville for bodyguards, to watch his latest special visitors. If not for him, these four would be alive now.

In fact, Boulard knew that their deaths were no great loss to the Republic of Seychelles. With the kind of men Malleville employed, no decent citizen was likely to be traumatized by their removal from the bright world of the living. They were thugs and petty criminals, some of them like Malleville himself, disgraced and hounded from the military or police force. Whatever the specific history of these four, Boulard didn't mourn for them.

Right now, he was more worried for himself.

When Colonel Roux found out about this latest incident, he would be furious. That in itself wasn't unusual, as the colonel was known for his explosive temper. The four dead weren't official personnel, and the shooting would eventually be explained away as some kind of a street crime. But it could have greater repercussions for Boulard.

He had been ordered to control the situation, put an end to the attacks, and he had told the colonel that it would be done. The four dead gunmen had been a part of his attempt to carry out his orders, but the plan had blown up in his face. From this point on, each shot fired in Victoria was one more bullet aimed at Ahriman Boulard's career. The best that he could hope for was a speedy end to the hostilities, and there were only two ways that could happen. One scenario had Gaetan Malleville's gunmen tracking down the foreigners responsible for the attacks and killing them. The other had a very different result.

Boulard didn't require a crystal ball to know which of the two solutions would be easier to realize. The stranger who had called him with an ultimatum earlier was bound to call again, demanding a response. It would be simple for the major to play along, give up the two most recent special visitors and tell the hit team where to go.

He had dispatched a car already to check out the property Afif Rahman had rented on the outskirts of Victoria. More men were posted at the Hotel Marcellais, prepared to call him if the fugitives returned, but Boulard considered that prospect unlikely. Stone and his associate knew they were hunted men, and they would go to ground as soon as possible. Without a list of independent contacts in the Seychelles, the house Rahman had leased was the most likely hiding place.

And once the stranger called again, once Boulard had told him where to find his prey, it would be simpler yet to reach out for Malleville and his hired killers, send them to the same address to mop up any stragglers who survived the firefight. Thus, Boulard could solve two problems at the same time, hopefully restore the colonel's faith in his ability to cope with an emergency, and thereby save himself.

More to the point, it had to work, because it was the only plan he had.

The hell of it was the waiting, never knowing when the stranger would call back. Boulard had left instructions at his office, ordering that any calls be forwarded to him, wherever he might be. Unfortunately he couldn't initiate the contact, and there was a chance—indeed, a likelihood—that more blood would be spilled before he got that crucial call. The hunters were determined that they shouldn't be refused, when they called back. They had no way of knowing that Boulard was ready to cooperate.

As if in answer to his very thoughts, one of his aides came forward hesitantly, offering a crisp salute when Boulard turned to face him.

"Sir," the young man said, "we have reports of other shootings."

Boulard could feel the hard knot in his stomach, twisting. It was all that he could do to keep a painful grimace from his face.

"Go on," he said.

"Two men are dead, both special visitors. One's name is Biko, from South Africa. The other was an Englishman. I think his name is Smith, sir."

Boulard didn't care about the names. He didn't even

care about the men, except as their demise affected him.
Two more nails in his coffin if he couldn't solve the problem soon, and there was nothing he could do to make the
damn intruders call him.

"Very well," Boulard replied, concealing his disgust,
the anguish that he felt. "We're finished here. Let's go
and see the rest."

MALLEVILLE WAS GROWING angrier with each stop on his
tour of the illicit weapons dealers in Victoria. Three
names remained for him to check, and so far none of those
whom he had questioned had been helpful in the least.
There was an outside chance that one of them had lied to
him, but he didn't think so. Each of them had been too
frightened of his wrath, and all had felt sufficient pain to
know what lay in store for them if he discovered they
were lying.

He believed them when they said that no one new had
come to them for weapons in the past two days. That still
left three more possibles before he had to rack his brain
and try to come up with a new approach. Some of the
pleasure boats that visited the Seychelles, he knew,
weren't closely examined by the staff at the marina. It
was always possible that someone had been bribed to
close his eyes or look the other way while guns were
brought ashore. That was another angle of attack, and one
Malleville would follow up if he learned nothing from the
last three dealers on his list.

It galled him that the search was taking him this long.
The security man took pride in getting swift results, en-
sured by his techniques and by the ruthless reputation he
had cultivated while he was employed as a police inspector in Victoria. Most of the city's criminals remembered
him, or if they were too young to have met him person-

ally, they had heard the stories of his violent nature from their elders.

Malleville knew that his notoriety had worked against him in the end. There were too many incidents on file, too many witnesses, and even though the scum he brutalized were usually too frightened to complain, he had grown cocky. He could admit it now. He had grown over-confident, convinced that no one could prevent him from dispensing justice in his own inimitable way.

And in a way, he had been right. They had dismissed him from the force, for all the good that did, but he was still in business, earning better pay in private life than he had ever done while wearing a policeman's uniform. Still working for the government, as well, though he was sure the politicians would be quick to disavow all knowledge of his unit if they should be questioned by the press. It hardly mattered, though. Reality was all that mattered to Malleville, and in the real world, he had freedom to perform as he had never done while he was drawing an official paycheck from the state.

Major Boulard and those above him had decided that the country should play host to human scum, if that scum had ability to pay. So be it. It wasn't his place to second-guess political decisions, even though he might denounce them privately while drinking with the handful of professionals he still considered friends. In order to protect its special visitors, the state required a special team to do the job, and Gaetan Malleville had been the first logical selection for an officer to lead that team. Now he had work to do, and legal niceties wouldn't deter him from completing his assignment.

By the fifth stop on his list, the shop and home of Philip Singh, Malleville was ready for a break. He didn't want to spend the night and most of the next day disrupting trade at the marina, butting heads with customs officers who could avoid his unofficial questions by referring him to their superiors. He wanted something now, and when Singh started lying to him, claiming he had sold no weapons in the past two weeks, Malleville experienced an almost gleeful feeling of relief.

"Two weeks, you say?" He smiled as if he had just won a million-dollar lottery.

"Two weeks, at least," Singh told him, nodding. "The business has been slow, Gaetan."

"I see."

The punch he threw came out of nowhere, smashing into Singh's left cheek with force enough to crack the bone. He watched the dealer fall, almost unconscious, nodding to a couple of his soldiers, waiting while they hauled the small man upright.

"You were never much at lying, Philip," Malleville told the groggy dealer. "For your own instruction, I will tell you that the secret of deception lies behind the eyes. Your eyes are shifty, nervous. You could not deceive a child with that expression on your face. It really needs more work."

Still smiling, Malleville kicked his prisoner between the legs, regarding him with casual interest as he tried to double over, failing even then, as the security men held him upright.

"Now," the ex–police inspector said, "we really need to have a little talk."

CHRIS STONE WAS hiding in the shadows of an alleyway across the street from Philip Singh's shop, when Malleville and his goons emerged. They took the little dealer with them, two men dragging him as if he were a broken mannequin, no fight left in him. He could barely hold his head up, much less walk, and there was no resistance as they tossed him bodily into the back seat of a black sedan.

Stone didn't know the men who carried Philip Singh away; their names were insignificant. He knew why they were there, and that was all that mattered. Someone in authority—Major Boulard, perhaps—was hunting him, attempting to outwit him and complete the job that had been bungled in the public square.

That ambush had been set up by Afif Rahman, however. Had the man from Hezbollah contrived some deal with the Seychelles authorities to give Stone up, and thus appease the hunters who were tearing up Victoria? It was a curious idea, but well within the realm of plausibility. And then again, it was entirely possible that the authorities were hunting both Rahman *and* Stone, the recent ambush merely an attempt on Rahman's part to dodge some of the heat. The only way that he could know for sure was if he got a chance to speak with Boulard, and Stone wasn't prepared to take that risk without some heavy firepower in hand—the kind of hardware Philip Singh kept in the basement of his shop.

Stone knew the layout from his two brief visits to the Singh establishment. It mattered little to him that the dealer had been dragged away; if anything, it stood to make things easier for the mercenary, since he wouldn't be asked to pay for any weapons he acquired. If Singh had relatives inside the building, or if the goon squad had left someone behind to watch for him, well, that was their bad luck. He still had the two Browning pistols, and he wouldn't hesitate to use them.

Hell, with all he had been through the past few hours, Stone was looking forward to the chance of shooting someone. Anyone. Just bring the bastards on.

He waited five more minutes, checking every shadow,

every doorway, for some sign of watchers. There was no one he could see, and so he finally crossed the street a half block down. He kept to the darkness where he could and reached the back door of the shop short moments later.

It was locked, but that wasn't a problem. Two swift kicks and he was in, a pistol in each hand, prepared to take all comers. No one challenged him, although he listened for the sounds a wife and children might produce upstairs. There was dead silence from that quarter, and it seemed the goons had left the shop unguarded in their haste to hustle Singh downtown.

He worked his way around the dimly lighted shop with caution, taking care that no one should be able to detect him from the street. A flight of stairs down to the basement was located behind a beaded curtain, and he walked down into darkness, keeping one gun pointed out ahead of him, the other raised and aimed back in the general direction he had come from, just in case. There was a light switch at the bottom of the stairs, and he flicked it, getting a clear view of the storeroom. No one was there to challenge him as he went shopping for a weapon to replace the mini-Uzi he had lost.

Singh kept his weapons in locked cabinets along the south wall of the storeroom. Sturdy padlocks held the doors shut tight, and Stone was forced to shoot them off when he couldn't find any tools with which to pry them loose. The echo of the gunshots nearly deafened him, and he stood at the bottom of the stairs for ten minutes afterward, expecting someone to investigate the noise.

But no one came.

It was a breeze from that point on. He chose a full-size Uzi with a threaded muzzle and a foot-long sound suppressor, spare magazines, already loaded, plus twelve boxes of 9 mm parabellum cartridges. He chose another suppressor to fit one of the Browning semiautos. Stone was leaning toward an AK-47 with a folding stock, as well, but he decided that it would be self-defeating if he took more guns than he could reasonably carry or employ. Beneath one cabinet, he found a canvas duffel bag to hold his latest acquisitions, filled it up and zipped it shut.

Stone already felt better as he left the shop. He kept one pistol out, the hammer cocked, as he emerged into the alleyway behind Singh's shop. When no one started to shoot at him, he decided he was free and clear. The idiots had missed their chance, and they would never have another opportunity to pin him down so easily.

He was sick of hiding out and dodging bullets. It was time for him to go on the offensive, show some nerve and take the battle to his enemies. But first, he needed information, and he knew just where to get it.

He would have a private little chat with Major Ahriman Boulard.

14

Major Boulard was growing nervous waiting for the call. In fact, he had begun to fear that the anonymous invader of his homeland wouldn't call him back. Suppose the people who stalked Afif Rahman and his American associate decided it was best if they simply continued killing in Victoria, until the city was reduced to chaos and there were no special visitors remaining to be found? What would become of Ahriman Boulard if all his efforts to prevent the violence came to naught?

Boulard didn't fear for his life, per se. There was no legal death penalty in the Republic of Seychelles, and failure to arrest an unknown fugitive wouldn't have been a criminal offense in any case. He wouldn't go to prison, but he might well be demoted, even banished from the military, under any one of several rules and regulations that permitted his superiors a wide discretion in their discipline of subordinates. His career would be ruined, and he could easily find himself unemployable in civilian life. Word of mouth would accomplish the rest, an unofficial blacklist that would leave him no choice but to flee— much as the hunted fugitives had come to the Seychelles, but in reverse.

Where would he go? Boulard had no idea, but he didn't intend to let things go that far. He still had the police, both military and civilian, scouring Victoria for any clue that would identify the man or men responsible for recent acts of violence. More importantly, in Boulard's view, he still had Gaetan Malleville and his collection of misfits, men who would not shrink from spilling blood in order to attain their goals.

And he still had the stranger's word.

The man had said he would call back, and something in Boulard's unquiet mind told him the caller hadn't lied. He *would* call back, because he wanted information only Boulard possessed. The various attacks that had occurred since they last spoke had been designed to sway the major, if nothing else—convince him that the stranger was in earnest, that he would wreak havoc in Victoria if he wasn't appeased.

Boulard was ready to accommodate him now, but he could only help the stranger—and himself—if someone dialed the telephone and asked for him by name. He couldn't reach out for the gunman on his own initiative. Dear God, it would have been so simple if he could! But he was forced to wait, shuttling around the town from one crime scene to another, staring at bodies and blood and destruction. Always waiting, hoping that the next call he received would not be Colonel Roux but the mysterious intruder who had turned Boulard's world upside down.

When he had time to think of other things, he wondered how his masters felt about their great decision now. Inviting wealthy fugitives from other countries to hide out in the Republic of Seychelles had been a gamble from the start, somebody's brainstorm that had balanced the potential income against worldwide criticism. It hadn't been terribly successful, and would clearly never challenge revenues from tourism in general, but the powers that be had voted to enshrine the program as a rule of law, defend it to the death—at least in theory—and defend their nation's right to welcome whom they chose, while charging whatever the market would bear.

Thus far, aside from certain peevish protests lodged with the United Nations, the Seychelles program for special visitors hadn't excited half the comment Boulard expected. The original announcement had been generally ignored in the United States and Europe, other than a single, brief report on CNN, and few civilians in the West knew anything about it. Boulard would have bet his pension, though, that many of them knew about the bloodshed in Victoria over the past twelve hours. *That* would make the news, if nothing else did, and the coverage would drag his country's reputation through the mud.

Such matters were beyond his power to control, however. Boulard had one specific mission, and thus far he had been failing miserably.

The small phone in his pocket cheeped at him insistently, a high-pitched tone as if a cricket were hidden somewhere on his person. Boulard snatched it from his pocket, nearly fumbled while unfolding it and somehow got it to his ear.

"Boulard."

It was his secretary calling. She had someone on the line, the same man who had called before, she thought, though he again refused to give his name. The major had commanded that—

"Yes, yes, I know my orders! Put him on for God's sake!"

Seconds later, after some metallic clicking sounds, he heard the grim, familiar voice. "Major Boulard?"

"I had begun to think you would not call me back." Boulard hoped that his nervousness would not be audible. "Have you got something for me?"

"As it happens, I do. It's been decided that I should

agree to your request for information in the interest of the greater good."

In fact, Boulard had come to that decision on his own, without consulting Colonel Roux or anybody else. It was another gamble, but he was prepared to take the risk.

"I'm listening," the stranger said.

"There is a house, outside Victoria..."

MALLEVILLE STUBBED OUT his cigarette and said, "Tell me again why you believe this trick will work."

"Because it's not a trick," Boulard replied. His tone and scrunched-up features telegraphed exasperation. "I gave him the actual directions to the house Afif Rahman has rented on the outskirts of the city. My surveillance officers confirm the Arab has arrived, together with another man whom they could not identify."

"The one called Stone, or Stevens," Malleville said.

"Presumably. The lookouts also spoke of several other men seen on the grounds."

"How many?" The security man's mind was working, trying to decide how many shooters he would need, and how much he should charge for pulling off a wholesale massacre.

"They counted five," Boulard replied. "Of course, it's possible there may be more unseen, inside the house."

"All armed," Malleville stated. He was talking to himself, but Boulard shrugged, as if he had become indifferent to the thought of gunfire in the streets.

"I'll take three dozen men," the ex-policeman added. "Allowing for the Arab's men and those you've sent to kill him, that should be enough."

Boulard didn't so much as flinch at the man's choice of words. You had to give him credit for that much, at least, a willingness to make the tough decisions, even if he kept his own hands scrupulously clean.

"I'm going with you," Boulard said, truly surprising Malleville for the first time in their years of casual acquaintance.

"That might not be such a good idea. There will be risk, and much...unpleasantness."

The major glared back at him. "I know the risk, and I have seen enough 'unpleasantness' tonight that nothing can surprise me anymore. I *will* be going with you, Gaetan."

"As for my men, Major..."

"They will continue under your command, of course. If I have any notions or suggestions, I will pass them on to you."

At that point, Malleville gladly would have spurned the job, but he had come too far for that. His questioning of gun dealers had singled out the man who armed the blond American, Chris Stone, but he had come no closer to the other men, those hunting Stone himself. Malleville was already committed to the chase and now, thanks to Boulard, he had an opportunity to wind it up by dawn. The hunters would go looking for Rahman and Stone, allowing the security force time to strike while they were otherwise engaged. As for the Arab and the blond American—

"What of the others?" Malleville asked.

"What others?" Boulard appeared confused.

"Rahman and Stone. The special visitors."

"Oh, *them*," Boulard replied as if he had forgotten all about the two men he was paid to save. "They have already caused us no end of embarrassment. I think it likely that whoever wanted them enough to take such drastic measures would prepare another team to hunt them down."

"It's possible, of course."

"Much better, then, if there is no one left for unknown enemies to hunt."

"You mean...?" Malleville knew exactly what the major meant but he wanted it spelled out in no uncertain terms.

"I mean," Boulard went on, "that it is best for all concerned if there are no survivors of tonight's last incident. It should appear that the intruders killed Rahman and Stone, along with such men as they hired to guard them, but that the attackers also died. Such things are not unknown."

"Indeed. I've seen it happen, when one side gets over-confident. Of course, ballistics—"

"Will not be a problem," Boulard assured him. "I will personally head up the investigation. The results will be as my superiors expect."

"In that case, by all means, let us proceed."

"Your men are ready?"

"Standing by," Malleville replied.

"All right." Boulard's face had gone blank. "Let's go."

The security man looked forward to the last act of the morbid drama, knowing that his men could use a decent workout. They had suffered from frustration since they started grilling weapons dealers, all to little result. The kind of men he had recruited lived for action, either on the battlefield or in the bedroom. Of the two, if they were forced to choose, Malleville believed that most of them would rather fight.

Now they would have their chance.

He only hoped three dozen guns would be enough to do the job.

THE TRICK OF FINDING someone who didn't wish to be found was knowing whom to ask. Chris Stone had made a solemn promise to himself that he would find Afif Rahman, punish the Arab for his treachery—but *how?* He couldn't ask their so-called chaperon, Major Boulard, for fear that he would tip Rahman. It was the Arab who had paid both of their entry fees, and Stone had no doubt that Boulard's first loyalty would lie with the initial money man.

And yet there had to be another way.

Audacity was called for, but he had to have a target first, before he could apply himself. If he could only think!

Boulard would know where Rahman went to ground—it was his job to know—but would he be the only one? It seemed unlikely, in a government bureaucracy designed to shelter fugitives for profit. Addresses and phone numbers would be recorded, bodyguards might be assigned to take the place of those who had been killed. It all meant paperwork, red tape, the delegation of authority. Boulard would have some kind of staff assigned to him, and someone would be working late to deal with the commotion in Victoria.

He found a public telephone, unscrewed the light bulb overhead, and started to make calls. It took three tries before he reached an office with a switchboard operator who not only recognized the name of Major Ahriman Boulard, but also knew the man. He wasn't in just now, but would the caller care to leave a message?

No, indeed.

Stone walked back several blocks to the Chevrolet sedan he had obtained by brute force. Its owner was a silent, lifeless bundle in the trunk, an old towel wrapped around his head to catch blood spilling from a single bullet wound behind one ear. As long as Stone obeyed the posted speed limits, he thought he would be fine. If he was stopped by the police for any reason, well, he had the Uzi on the seat beside him, covered with a newspaper, ready to rock and roll.

He found the office building he was looking for. A sign out front informed him that the Ministry of Tourism and Commerce had its offices inside. He parked around in back, locked up the stolen car and took the keys. Beneath his arm, one of the Browning pistols rode in fast-draw leather, muzzle heavy with its sound suppressor.

It was no great trick getting into Boulard's building. Even with the recent spate of violence in Victoria there were no guards in sight. Stone understood the mind-set well enough: there had been no attacks upon the government, so why should any guards be posted at a government facility?

Thank God for idiots, he thought, and made his way inside, found the directory and took a waiting elevator to the second floor. Stone wasn't sure what he hoped to find or learn at Boulard's office; he was playing it by ear, and hoped that something would occur to him before he wasted too much precious time. It wouldn't do to have the major walk in on him while he was attempting to retrieve an address for Rahman.

Stone had expected several people in the office, but he found one man alone at the reception desk. The doors to several other offices were closed, with no light showing underneath. The merc swallowed hard as he pushed through the doorway, settling on a fair approximation of a German accent as he spoke.

"Good evening," he addressed the startled man behind the desk, flashing a phony German passport in his face as if it were a badge. "I am Inspector Heinrich Klempt, with

Interpol. I am, unfortunately, late for an appointment with your Major—ah, what is his name?—Boulard.''

The man behind the desk was blinking at him. "Ah. Major Boulard has gone, sir.''

"Yes, of course, he would have gone. I'm late, you see. My flight, and then, oh, well, it can't be helped. I was supposed to help him with the Palestinian. You know the name, Afif Rahman?''

The young man hesitated, swallowing, his Adam's apple bobbing. He was clearly undecided as to how he should respond, his very hesitancy telling Stone that he was onto something.

"Well, man? Have you lost your tongue! This is important and official business!" When pretending to be German, throw your weight around and add an extra dash of arrogance. It was expected, and it seldom failed.

"Major Boulard has gone to see the man you speak of," the receptionist acknowledged. "I should call and ask—''

"By all means, call him," Stone said, interrupting. "I am sure he will appreciate your adding to the unavoidable delay in my arrival at the scene.''

The receptionist's hand froze halfway to the telephone, poised in midair, then retreated to rest on the desktop, fingers drumming nervously. "You are from Interpol?''

"That is correct. It is essential that I see the major now, before he makes a grave mistake that could endanger his career.''

The young receptionist made up his mind. "He left an address where he could be reached in case of an emergency.''

"This clearly qualifies.''

The young man rattled off a street name and a number, neither one of which meant anything to Stone. He glowered back at his informant, asking for directions, and the young man grabbed a notepad, sketching out a simple map of major streets that led to the outskirts of Victoria.

"Ah, yes, I see. Most helpful. Thank you." Stone was almost to the door when he appeared to have another thought. He turned back toward the young man at the desk and saw him reaching for the telephone once more. "What are you doing?" he inquired.

"I will be pleased to tell the major you are coming."

"That won't be necessary," Stone informed him, giving up the accent as he drew his silenced Browning, squeezing off two quick shots from a dozen feet away.

The man toppled over backward in his desk chair, sprawling on the vinyl-covered floor. He was invisible from where his killer stood. As a precaution, Stone reached down and turned the simple latch that would secure the door behind him when it closed. The lock wouldn't stop anyone who had a key, but from the late receptionist's behavior when Stone entered, no one was expected at that hour of the night.

Soon Stone would have both Rahman and the major, and he would have revenge. As he retraced his steps and rode the elevator down, then walked back to his waiting vehicle, he found that he could hardly wait.

But overeagerness could get him killed if he went rushing into a potentially explosive situation with his guard down, focused on the sweet taste of revenge instead of plotting out his moves. He was a soldier first, an absolute professional, and he would take it one step at a time.

All good things come to those who wait.

But in his heart, Chris Stone still felt that he had waited long enough.

"THE MEN ARE READY?"

"As you say," Muhammad Alhazred replied. "I've

spoken to each one of them myself.''

''All right, then.'' Even as he spoke the words and tried to make himself relax by force of will alone, Rahman couldn't escape a feeling that they had forgotten something, left some small precaution unaccounted for. It was a nagging sense of apprehension, much like helplessness, which made him want to scream and smash his fist into the walls until his knuckles bled.

Enough of that!

Rahman was known for icy self-control, regardless of the circumstances, and he wouldn't now allow himself the luxury of temper tantrums. Alhazred watched him with the flat eyes of a reptile, waiting for his orders, counting on Rahman to know what should be done in any given situation. Weakness was a cancer that would finish him with Hezbollah. A show of indecision was the signature on his death warrant.

''They must take no action without my direct authority,'' Rahman told his subordinate, ''unless we are attacked. Make sure they understand.''

''I will.''

''You trust these men?''

Alhazred shrugged. ''They were the best available.''

''See to them, then.''

The best available, he echoed in his mind, and scowled at the idea. The men Alhazred had recruited were no more than common thugs. They didn't know whom they were working for, nor did they care as long as they were paid in cash, with extra rental charges for the weapons they supplied. Their fees were reasonable in the circumstances, even though the unexpected payment left Rahman more than a little short of cash. When it was daylight, and the banks were open, he would have to venture out again, arrange a wire transfer from one of his accounts to keep himself in pocket money.

And before that happened, he would have to make it through the night alive.

It was two hours now, and counting, since the failed attempt to kill Chris Stone. Rahman felt better now that he was safely hidden from his enemies, although it would have helped to know that Stone was dead. He didn't like the notion of the ruthless mercenary stalking him, but there was little he could do about it at the moment. Stone was on unfamiliar ground, had no idea where he had gone and *he* was being hunted, too. With any luck, the men who wanted Stone would find him soon and finish it, before Rahman had any more cause for concern.

And what of their interest in him? Rahman's last conversation with Boulard had made it crystal clear that someone on the other team was after Stone's employer, even if they didn't have a name or nationality to work from. How long would it be until the nervous local government decided to play ball, as the Americans would say, and sell him out? The sooner he could get away from the Republic of Seychelles, the better he would like it, but he couldn't go tonight, perhaps not for another day or two, until he made arrangements for his transportation in another name.

Two million dollars down the drain, and counting. It was an unconscionable waste of money when he studied it in retrospect, but how could he have known they would be followed halfway around the world? It was preposterous to think that anyone from the United States could track them, much less that Americans would try to kill them without warning in a neutral country. And because it was unthinkable, the plan had very nearly worked.

Rahman was smarter than the Yankees, though. They

knew it now, and he could almost feel the venom of their hatred, so much like his own. Perhaps, in fifty years or so, when they had learned to hate for generations, as the outcast Palestinians had learned to do, the soft men of the West would be his equal. By that time, of course, Afif Rahman would be long dead. The struggle would have passed to other, younger hands. It would be someone else's turn to bear the torch of everlasting holy war.

For now, however, he was in a battle for survival, facing unknown enemies, with common thugs employed in his defense. It was a situation that would bear close watching, and Rahman wasn't a man to leave his life, his future, in the hands of someone else when he could do the job himself.

He only prayed to God that the matter would be settled soon, and that he could be on his way.

15

The house was large and massive, separated from its nearest neighbors by an eight-foot wall surrounding wooded grounds, perhaps three acres in extent. It was a legacy of colonial times in Victoria, when the capital of the Seychelles was named for England's queen, and British businessmen controlled the island chain with aid from soldiers dressed in pith helmets and scarlet coats. Remodeled slightly after independence, it had managed to avoid the fate of many other mansions in the new republic, which were subdivided into instant housing projects for the poor. It was a rental property now, its tenant one Afif Rahman, of Hezbollah.

Bolan approached the house in darkness, dressed in black, his face and hands smeared with the same cosmetics used by soldiers everywhere when they were called upon to hunt by night. He could have used an M-16 or a Kalashnikov, but there was none available, so Bolan made the best of what he had. The sleek Beretta Model 92-S was slung beneath his left arm, while the MP-5 K submachine gun hung across his back. Grenades and extra magazines were clipped to his belt or carried in a bandolier across his chest. For extra firepower, he also carried the Galil rifle, its stock and bipod folded, with the sound suppressor and Nimrod telescopic sight removed. The piece would fire only in semiauto mode, but that was fair enough in the Executioner's hands, and it had stopping power equal to an AK-47.

It would have to do.

He scouted the perimeter, searching for guards outside the wall and finding none. When he had found a handy tree and scrambled to a perch among its branches, he could see that there was no barbed wire or other obvious security devices on the flat top of the wall. No sound or other indication of patrolling dogs, though it was possible that he had missed them in the darkness. He could see the house, with lights showing, and knew where he had to go. Between his perch and Bolan's destination, solitary sentries found their way around the grounds with flashlights, making no attempt to hide.

Or were they simply a diversion? Bait for a potential prowler?

There was only one way to find out.

He timed the move, scoped out his landing zone as best he could, then ran along a sturdy limb that pointed roughly toward the house and launched himself into thin air. It was a drop of twelve or thirteen feet, and Bolan landed in a crouch, as he had been instructed back in boot camp many lifetimes earlier. It was impossible to make the jump without some noise, from rustling leaves behind him to the sound of impact on the grass, but no one seemed to notice. The warrior counted off ninety seconds before he rose and started to move toward the lighted house.

He had a short list of essential targets in his mind. Two men, in fact, would be enough to satisfy his quest: Chris Stone and the fanatic who had hired him to unleash a reign of terror in the States. Bolan wasn't familiar with the name supplied by Ahriman Boulard, but simply knowing that the man was Hezbollah provided all the background information he required. Techniques and personalities aside, when you have seen one Arab terrorist, you've seen them all.

Leaving the rifle slung across his shoulder, Bolan drew the Beretta. He didn't want to rouse the palace guard before he reached the house if he could help it. With experience and skill, perhaps a little luck, it should be possible to come within striking distance of his prey before he revealed himself. He hoped so, anyway.

But luck had turned against him, as it happened. Fifty yards inside the wall, he was proceeding toward his target when a shadow moved on his left. Someone spoke to him in French, immediately trying him in English when the first attempt brought no response.

"Who is that?"

Bolan swiveled toward the voice, his gun hand rising, the Beretta an extension of himself. He stroked the trigger twice, heard bullets striking flesh and saw the shadow slumping backward with a muffled cry.

And as he fell, the dead man squeezed the trigger on his submachine gun, spraying bullets toward the waxing moon, and he made noise enough to wake the dead.

GUNFIRE!

Afif Rahman had grown up with the sound, and it had held no terrors for him since he was a child. In truth, he couldn't say that he was frightened now, but he was worried. Definitely. This place was supposed to be secure, his sanctuary, yet someone had discovered him, and only hours after his attempt to kill Christopher Stone had failed.

So be it.

He picked up the Beretta Model 12, a submachine gun whose design had made it popular for use in futuristic science-fiction films, although the gun had been in use since 1958. Chambered in 9 mm parabellum, it weighed just over eight pounds with a loaded 32-round magazine in place, and the stubby foregrip provided extra control when firing in full-automatic mode, with a cyclic rate of 500 to 550 rounds per minute. Less popular with professional soldiers than either the Uzi or the German MP-5, it was a compact and efficient weapon all the same.

Alhazred burst into the room just as Rahman was moving toward the exit. "We have contact," he informed his leader.

"And I have ears. The men?"

"I'm going to them now. I wanted to be certain that—"

"I'm fine," Rahman assured him. "Go, now. I will join you in a moment."

The younger man bolted from the room, and Rahman waited for a moment, giving his assistant time to join the gunmen he had hired as guards.

He wondered if they would be good enough to frustrate an attack upon the house. More to the point, he wondered *who* was staging the attack. Was it the same man who had hunted Stone in the United States and Mexico? Did he possess the skill and wherewithal to follow them halfway around the world? Or was it Stone himself this time, intent on payback for the ambush in Victoria?

It would be helpful if Rahman was able to identify his enemy, but it wasn't essential. All he really had to do was stay alive until Alhazred or one of their hired guns got lucky, finished the intruder with a clean shot to the head or heart. Of course, if there was more than one intruder on the grounds, the kill would be more difficult. Rahman was equally prepared to fight or flee, whichever option seemed to hold the better prospect for his own survival.

He wasn't a coward, and would readily have executed

any man who called him one, but growing up as a guerrilla fighter with the *fedayeen* had taught him that there were certain times to make your stand, become a martyr for the cause, and there were other times when it was best to disengage from contact with the enemy, survive to fight another day. His dying here, in the Republic of Seychelles, a hunted man, would do no good for Hezbollah or Rahman's lifelong war against Israel. If anything, it would do harm, portraying one of Hezbollah's chief operators as a frightened animal, tracked down and slaughtered in a hideout far from home.

Better that he escape, return to join his brothers in the Middle East and help to prepare a story that would cover any leaks of his involvement in America, in Mexico, in the Seychelles. If he was known, if his role in the spate of violence should be publicized, Rahman would be available for PR and damage control.

First, though, he had to make it out of the Seychelles alive, out of this house, which could become a death trap if he wasn't very careful.

Flicking off the submachine gun's safety, thumbing its selector switch to automatic fire, Rahman opened the study door and stepped into the outer hallway. He heard firing from the grounds outside and recognized the sound of several different weapons—a Kalashnikov, at least one pistol, two or three 9 mm SMGs. That fire was concentrated, for the moment, at the east—or front—side of the manor house. Accordingly he headed west, in the direction of the back door and detached garage outside.

It would be foolish to attempt a getaway on foot, and no one in his right mind ever called Afif Rahman a fool. At least, no one who was alive today.

He would escape the trap, if Allah willed it, and he just might find an opportunity to kill one of his enemies along the way. In any case, his hours in the Republic of Seychelles were numbered, and his next priority—after escape from the besieged estate—would have to be evacuation of the island state itself.

Good riddance.

Moving swiftly toward the back door of the house, Rahman could hardly wait.

CHRIS STONE WAS straddling the eight-foot wall, preparing for a drop into the shrubbery below, when suddenly all hell broke loose. It started with a burst of submachinegun fire, 9 mm by the sound, and people started shouting after that, converging with flashlights on the spot where they believed the sound had come from. An assault rifle was next to open up, the unmistakable Kalashnikov, and it degenerated into general firing after that.

He took advantage of the diversion, dropping from his perch atop the wall and moving toward the lighted house at double-time. He didn't have a clue to what was happening, but he could guess. Someone besides himself had come after Rahman, and it was fifty-fifty as to who that someone would turn out to be: a hit team from the Seychelles government, or someone from the States.

Belasko? Could he be that lucky?

Even as the thought took shape, Stone felt a little chill of fear that was at odds with his surroundings, wholly foreign to the muggy, tropical climate. This Belasko character had followed Stone from Idaho to Baja California, then back again to Florida, but would he honestly show up in the Seychelles, halfway around the world? If so, it was an opportunity for Stone to even up the score on all accounts, Belasko *and* Rahman. He could repay both men at once, for screwing up the sweetest deal he'd ever had since he went private, selling his services as a mercenary soldier.

Or he might just get his ass kicked straight into a shallow grave.

Screw that, Stone thought, and forged ahead through semidarkness, following the lights and sounds of combat that were leading him inexorably toward the house. Some place Rahman had here, not quite a palace, but it was the next best thing. The lap of luxury, for damn sure. Stone was curious to know what some of Rahman's friends in Hezbollah would think about his home away from home in the Seychelles while they were living hand to mouth in tents or shanties thrown together out of salvaged lumber, tar paper and cardboard.

The sounds of combat from the far side of the house had drawn most of Rahman's hired bodyguards in that direction, but Stone met a straggler on his way. The man was young, perhaps midtwenties, and he seemed scared to death. The guy was bailing out, taking the path of least resistance, running from the fight...except that now, bad luck had brought the fight to him.

Stone used the Browning pistol with the sound suppressor attached. One shot, dead center in the chest, was all it should have taken. You could tell the guy was dead or getting there, the blank expression on his face and all that blood, but he kept standing there, as if a gorgon's glance had turned him into stone. Three seconds. Four.

Stone shot him in the forehead to accelerate the process, and the impact of the second bullet took his target down. Unable to resist a hardware upgrade, Stone relieved the dead man of his AK-47 and the three spare magazines he carried in a canvas belt pouch. They would stretch his pockets out of shape, but Stone wanted the extra firepower. He had a feeling he would need it.

Brief moments later, Stone had his first clear view of the house since he had jumped down from the wall on the perimeter. One man had been detailed to guard the main door, and while he should have been alert to any movement at the tree line, the young man had his back turned toward the darkness, staring at the southeast corner of the house, from which the sounds of combat seemed to emanate.

Again, Stone took advantage of a lucky break. He couldn't say if there was anyone behind the windows facing his position, whether someone in the house would open up on him when he emerged from cover, but he had to take that chance. Rahman was in the house, and that was all that mattered to him at the moment.

There was no safe and easy way across the open lawn. Stone left the shadows of the tree line, sprinting toward the manor house, the captured AK-47 leveled at his target.

The gunman heard him coming somehow, but by that time Stone had closed the gap to less than thirty yards. He saw the young man pivot, hands white knuckled where they gripped an Uzi SMG, eyes wide with fright.

The difference between a true professional and a pretender was the willingness to kill without a second thought or fleeting hesitation. Some of that came with experience, but most of it was drawn from somewhere in the man himself. You were either an efficient killer or you weren't.

Stone was.

A short burst from his AK struck the sentry in the chest and slammed him back against the nearest stucco wall. The quantities of blood erupting from his wounds told the merc the sentry wasn't wearing body armor, and the glazed eyes reassured him that the man was dead before he fell, without firing a shot.

Stone doubted that his own brief contribution to the general racket would be audible to soldiers locked in combat on the far side of the house, but he was short on time and not about to take that chance. A second AK burst ripped through the front door's locking mechanism, just in case it had been latched behind the lookout, and he shouldered through into the house.

"Honey," he said to no one in particular, "I'm home."

ONE OF MALLEVILLE'S pet peeves was showing up late for a party. Sometimes it was fashionable, even mandatory, to arrange and orchestrate an entrance that would leave the others gaping, but it galled him even so to think that someone else was first at the champagne, the caviar and canapés, the women.

Or the killing.

There had been no help for it this time, of course. Boulard had only tipped him half an hour ago, and it had taken time for him to recall three dozen soldiers from the streets, see to their weapons, load them into vehicles and point them in the right direction.

Malleville was riding in the back seat of the second car, Boulard beside him, looking nervous, chewing on his lower lip. Why had he come along when anyone could see that he was only in the way? Some kind of test, the security man decided, or perhaps he simply didn't trust the men to do their jobs. Whatever, he could still be useful if and when the regular police showed up, to cover for Malleville and his commandos.

If Boulard survived that long.

"You're armed?" Malleville asked.

The major raised a hand to pat the left side of his coat. "Of course."

A pistol only, then. Malleville reached down between

his feet and drew a loaded Uzi from the bulging duffel bag. "Take this," he said, handing it over. "Just in case."

Boulard accepted it and held the weapon in his lap. By then they were within a few blocks of their destination, and the point car radioed a message back. "Gunfire ahead."

Malleville heard nothing, but he pressed a button in the armrest at his elbow, lowering the power window, hissing at his soldiers to be quiet. There it was, the pop-crack-bang of small-arms fire. No doubt about it—they were late.

There was a walkie-talkie in each car, and he spoke to all of them at once. "The party has begun without us," he declared, "but we are going in regardless. Keep your guns clear and your asses down."

Before any of his commandos could respond, Malleville addressed the point car's driver. "Eric, if the gates are open when we get there, drive on through. If not, it makes no difference. Break them down. You understand?"

The driver's voice came back at him. "Yes, Gaetan."

The burly ex-policeman felt a sudden rush, excitement surging through him at the prospect of some solid action. He enjoyed this part of it, the violence. His second wife, in one of her unruly moods, had told him that he lived to brutalize his fellow man. He suspected she was right.

Malleville checked his own Uzi to make sure the magazine was seated properly and that it had a live round in the chamber. When he set the safety, he felt compelled to flick it back and forth repeatedly to make sure it wouldn't stick. It was a nervous habit, granted, but it never paid to take machinery for granted when your life was riding on the line.

The lead car braked, then swung into the entrance of a driveway, pointed toward a wrought-iron gate and rapidly accelerated. They could have used more speed, but even so, the full weight of the limousine burst through the gates and pushed them back with a tremendous screeching sound, as paint was flayed from both sides of the car.

There was a flash of gunfire from the left, a manic strobe effect, as someone crouching in the bushes opened fire. The men in the point car were returning it with interest, pouring rounds into the shrubbery that could conceal a man but would offer him no real protection in a firefight. By the time Malleville's own car cleared the gate, the threat was neutralized, a pair of legs protruding from behind a tattered-looking hedge.

The five-car caravan proceeded toward the house, where the security man reckoned they would find the men he sought. Who else had found them in the meantime? Would he also meet the men, presumably Americans, who had been raising hell around Victoria the past twelve hours?

He hoped so. It would be a pleasure to solve all his problems at a single stroke. Such an achievement ought to rate a bonus when the time came for him and his loyal troopers to be paid.

But first, there was a battle to be won, a nice warm bloodbath to be savored.

WHATEVER HAPPENED NEXT, Ahriman Boulard knew he couldn't let them know he was afraid. The major wasn't a combat veteran—the Republic of Seychelles had never fought a war—but he was trained, at least in theory, to survive and triumph under fire. As for reality...

He felt his heart skip when the limo coasted to a halt, the doors sprang open and the security force started to pile out to go in search of human targets. Boulard followed them, albeit grudgingly, because he dared not sit there by himself. It would humiliate him if he froze now; it would mark him as a coward. Worse, it just might get him killed.

Safety in numbers, he repeated to himself as he ducked low and scuttled after Malleville. No one was shooting at them yet, as far as he could tell, but that would change as soon as they engaged the enemy.

And who, exactly, *was* the enemy?

The fighting had begun before they reached the villa, so there had to be two teams of antagonists at least. He guessed that it would be Rahman and Stone against the nameless men who had pursued them from the States and wreaked such havoc in Victoria. The men whom he, Boulard, had guided to this very spot in hopes that he would catch them all together, kill two buzzards with a single stone.

Now that his wish was coming true, the major almost regretted making it, afraid that it would backfire, rebound to his everlasting detriment. How pitifully ironic it would be if he was killed, or even gravely wounded, in a mantrap of his own design.

A dead man sprawled across the front porch of the great house, lying in a pool of blood so dark it looked like thick raspberry syrup. Just beyond his body, the front door was standing open, pocked with bullet holes around the knob and dead bolt. Malleville whistled sharply, aimed a hand in the direction of the porch, four fingers rigidly extended, and a quartet of his gunmen left the jogging column, mounting stairs to penetrate the house.

He knew the game, Boulard thought, and knew that he was fortunate to be with killers at a time and place where killing was required. How grim it would have been if *he* had been in charge of the attack, so frightened now that he could barely put one foot before the other and continue moving toward the raucous sounds of battle. A carping voice in Boulard's mind still nagged at him to run away, protect himself, but he ignored it with an effort, following Malleville and hoping that the bullets, when they came, would strike at someone else before they cut him down.

They reached a corner of the house, beyond the porch of death, and one of Malleville's scouts leaned out to check the action. He ducked back again and whispered something to his leader, after which Malleville turned to Boulard.

"We've got them," he declared. "No more than six or seven on the one side, dueling with some others in the trees. Our best chance is to hit them hard before they realize we're here."

"As you think best," Boulard replied.

Malleville grinned at him, a knowing smile that made Boulard wish he could kill the ex-policeman where he stood. "Come on, then," the security-force leader said, raising his voice so all of his troops could hear him. "Do you want to live forever?"

And Boulard felt close to weeping as he joined the rush around the corner. Thinking desperately to himself that yes, he did.

SOMETIMES A FIGHT came down to numbers, while at other times it hinged solely on a warrior's skill. Most battles were a combination of both elements.

Like now.

The force defending Bolan's target wasn't large. In fact, he saw no more than six or seven guns before him as he reached the tree line, but the men fanned out professionally, dropping prone and covering the woods from which the early burst of automatic fire had come, alerting them to danger. If he started sniping at them now with the Galil, his first shot would reveal him to the others, and it took only one soldier with a steady hand, one lucky shot to bring him down.

The other way was risky, too, but Bolan felt obliged to try.

He palmed one of the frag grenades and primed it, winding up the pitch. He lobbed it toward the center of the line, throwing from well back in the shadows of the tree line, hoping it would do the trick.

Four seconds and a fraction elapsed, before the apple green grenade went off behind the opposition lineup. No one was disabled by the blast, but it was meant as a diversion, and it served that function well enough. Since no one on the firing line had seen him make the pitch, a sudden detonation on their flank surprised the gunners, made them scramble, several of them turning back to see if someone was attacking from behind.

It was the moment Bolan had been waiting for, the edge he needed. The Galil was at his shoulder when the grenade went off, and there was no need for the Nimrod scope at that range. Using open sights, he pegged the gunner nearest to the center of the line and slammed a 7.62 mm bullet through his chest as he was rising to one knee, attempting to protect himself against a flanking strike.

Too late.

Bolan was shifting to his left before the first man dropped, acquiring target number two and squeezing off another round. A head shot this time, ripping through the gunman's lower jaw with force enough to snap his neck. The rag-doll figure toppled over backward, squirming briefly on the bloodstained grass before he gave it up, relaxing into death.

A couple of the others had him spotted now, unloading

with their automatic weapons, coming close enough that
Bolan had to dodge and find new cover. From the corner
of his eye, he thought he saw more soldiers breaking from
the house, filling the gaps that he had opened in the line.
How many reinforcements did they have in there? More
to the point, how many could he kill, now that they had
him spotted, hosing down the trees with automatic fire?

He poked his rifle through an insubstantial screen of
ferns, prepared to take one shot and scramble for his life
before they had a chance to zero on his muzzle-flash. Bolan was scanning for a target when he heard a shout, another burst of gunfire and *more* soldiers charged into the
battle from the other side, to the northwest. There was a
minimum of twenty-five or thirty new arrivals, and he felt
his spirits plunge. It took a heartbeat for the Executioner
to grasp that these men weren't attacking him, but rather
firing on the outnumbered defenders of the house.

The Bible said that he who hesitated was lost, and that
was every bit as true in combat as in matters of the soul.
Bolan didn't waste time attempting to discover who his
benefactors were. He simply took advantage of the moment, surging to his feet and running back along the tree
line, looking for an angle of approach that stood a halfway
decent chance of bringing him to cover on the far side of
the house.

There was no safety there, no safety anywhere, but he
still had to seek his enemies, since they weren't about to
come to him. The curious diversion was the last he could
expect, and Bolan didn't mean to waste it.

Running with his head down, knees and elbows pumping, the Executioner broke from cover, sprinting in a zig-
zag line toward the detached garage.

16

It should have been so easy, wiping out the stragglers on the lawn and moving on from there to take the house. Gaetan Malleville had seen it in his mind's eye, step by bloody step, his enemies collapsing under concentrated automatic fire, dying like rats, with only minimal resistance in the face of overwhelming force.

It took him by surprise, then, when the six or seven gunners on the lawn cut loose with everything they had. He was amazed to see two men go down in front of him, immediately followed by a third and a fourth.

Malleville was cursing as he fell prone on the grass, his Uzi almost slipping from his fingers. He couldn't remember the decision to prostrate himself, although it may have saved his life. Disoriented for a moment, he wondered if he could have tripped, then he felt the rush of warm blood soaking through his trousers, from a deep wound in his thigh.

What was happening? He had been shot before, a graze across his ribs, but never anything like this. He knew enough anatomy to place the major arteries and understand that he was gravely injured. How long did it take to bleed to death?

Not long.

Enraged, Malleville leveled his SMG at the retreating gunmen and unloaded the whole magazine in one long burst. The muzzle-flash prevented him from seeing whether any of his rounds struck home, but he had other, more immediate concerns in mind.

He rolled over on his left side, fumbling with his belt buckle. It seemed to take forever, but he got it open, started tugging on the belt to free it, rolling first this way, then the other, as it wriggled through his belt loops.

Glancing up as he began to wrap the makeshift tourniquet around his thigh, he saw Boulard regarding him with an expression that was somewhere in between surprise and simple curiosity. The major made no move to help him, and Malleville wasn't surprised. The brass were only good at looking out for number one.

His hands were slippery with blood now, and he had trouble with the belt buckle as he prepared to cinch the tourniquet. A wave of dizziness almost defeated him, his fingers loosening their grip so that the belt went slack, fresh jets of blood exploding from his mangled leg. His pants were soaked in it, the grass beneath him blackened in the moonlight.

His slick hands found a new grip on the belt and pulled it tighter as he slumped back on the lawn. Around him, the explosive sounds of battle sounded small and distant now, as if the fighting had moved on and left him in its wake, forgotten with the newly dead.

It had been years since Malleville set foot in a church, but now he crossed himself with one hand, while his other gripped the tourniquet. In whispers, dredging up forgotten phrases from his childhood, he began to pray.

THE HOUSE WAS relatively quiet, even with the storm of gunfire rattling away outside. Chris Stone wasn't sure where he should look first in his hunt for Afif Rahman. The sneaky bastard could be anywhere, even outside the

villa with his men, but something told Stone that his
quarry would avoid the thick of battle if he could.

Where to begin?

His train of thought was interrupted by a blur of movement on the landing overhead. Stone swung around in that
direction, tracking with his Uzi, as a swarthy gunman
started blasting at him with an M-1 carbine. It was the
merc's good fortune that the gunner rushed the first shot,
missed his target by at least two feet and blew a tall ce-
ramic vase to smithereens.

Before the shooter could correct his aim, Stone was in
motion, breaking toward the staircase, firing as he went.
The Uzi sputtered through its suppressor, short bursts of
parabellum shockers chipping divots from the stucco wall
beside his adversary, crimson mist replacing plaster dust
as bullets found their mark. The shooter staggered backward, pumping wild rounds toward the ceiling in a reflex
action as he fell.

Stone made up his mind to search the second floor instead of prowling through the rooms downstairs. It was a
mental coin toss, and the second story won. If nothing
else, he could make sure that there was no one else up
there, about to snipe him when his back was turned.

The mercenary had barely reached the landing where
his latest kill reposed when four men burst in through the
front door of the house. He didn't recognize their faces,
but the weapons in their hands were as familiar to the
mercenary as old friends. Two had AK-47s, while the
other pair carried French-made submachine guns, the
MAT 49s.

Stone was outgunned, but the intruders hadn't seen him
yet. He had perhaps two seconds, and he used the fleeting
time to his advantage, dropping to a crouch and aiming
through the space between two banisters. How many

rounds remained in the Uzi's magazine? There was no time to check, or even guess, if Stone intended to survive.

He held down the submachine gun's trigger and swung its muzzle in an arc from left to right and back again. A storm of parabellum slugs ripped through his targets, catching them before they recognized their danger, only one of them so much as glancing up before the bullets tore his face away. It was a massacre, but Stone knew he was lucky, that it could as easily have gone the other way.

Reloading swiftly, he was thankful for the Uzi's suppressor, which had apparently prevented those outside from knowing that a second battle had been joined inside the house. If these four had been on their toes, a trifle more alert to danger, Stone would be a dead man now, a stranger's hands inside his pockets, trying to discover who he was and what had brought him here.

He moved along the upstairs hallway, checking the doors on each side. Most opened easily and showed him empty rooms. The two doors he found locked, he kicked in and crossed the threshold in a crouched rush, discovering that they were set aside as storage space.

Nothing.

Stone was getting nervous, risking a surprise each time he cleared a room and came back to the central corridor. It was a fluke, he thought, that no one had discovered him so far and sounded the alarm.

The last room, on the west side of the house, was sparsely furnished, but it had the feel of recent occupation. Stone could smell tobacco smoke; he saw two glasses standing on a polished coffee table, one of them containing dregs of amber fluid. Up close, it smelled like whiskey. Someone had been here, all right, but he or they had left, no telling when. He could have missed them by a heartbeat, or by hours.

Moving to the window, Stone kept to the shadows as he peered outside. There was no point in giving anyone a target if he could avoid it. From his vantage point, he saw two bodies on the lawn, stretched out perhaps ten feet apart, both leaking blood from what he knew were bullet wounds. The main action was somewhere to his right, beyond his line of sight, but there was…what?

A solitary figure ran hard for the detached garage, a man who could have been—no, wait. The runner turned to glance behind him.

Afif Rahman was making for the cars. He had a major lead already, and if Stone didn't hurry the Arab would get away. If he escaped Stone this time, it would be impossible to track him down again.

Stone cursed his wretched luck and sprinted back in the direction of the stairs.

BOLAN HAD HOPED he could avoid the main brunt of the fighting, but it wasn't working out. The latest soldiers to arrive were tying up a portion of the home-defense team, but they wouldn't score an easy victory. More gunmen were emerging from the mansion, and a couple of the downstairs windows had been broken out by snipers, muzzle-flashes winking in the night. Bolan was glad for the diversion that had saved his life, but the chaotic battle now in progress didn't help his chances of a search inside the house.

Still, if the men he sought were in there, the Executioner had to find a way to root them out.

He was advancing cautiously upon a patio with sliding doors, attempting to avoid the glare of two surviving floodlights, when the battle raging on the east lawn gained a new dimension of confusion. Someone from the home team had appropriated one of the crew wagons parked out front, and now the vehicle was charging toward its former occupants, horn blaring, flashers blinking, while the headlights glared on high beams. As he watched, the massive car began to swerve erratically, tires clawing at the lawn and leaving mangled turf behind as it careered from one potential target to the next.

The starboard fender clipped one gunman as he tried to dodge, too late, and set him spinning like a top before he fell. A second gunman stood his ground, unloading with a semiautomatic rifle, but his bullets couldn't crack the tinted windshield. By the time he changed his mind and tried to run, the juggernaut was on him, slamming him to the earth and rolling over him as if he were a speed bump made of chuck roast.

Guns on every side were blasting at the car now, chipping paint away in abstract patterns, but the bullets didn't penetrate. Whoever paid to have the limo armor plated had received his money's worth and then some. Even pumping lead into the tires got no result, since they were puncture proof, designed—and priced—specifically for presidents, prime ministers and anybody else for whom an unexpected blowout could mean sudden death. They could have stopped the limo with a range of armor-piercing HE shells or rockets, none of which was readily available, but as it was, the driver had a free run of the battlefield.

Until the stupid bastard rolled his window down.

It was an act of madness, wholly inexplicable, and Bolan didn't even try to read the driver's mind. One moment, men were dodging every which way to avoid the limousine, and then the driver started firing through his window with a pistol, spotting targets on the run as if he had grown tired of simply playing bumper tag. It was the chance his enemies had waited for, and several of them opened fire at once. The tinted glass didn't reveal what happened when their bullets struck, but Bolan saw the limo lose momentum, veering aimlessly off track and rolling to a halt. A nearby shooter picked himself up off the grass, ran over to the car and emptied half a magazine from his MAT 49 SMG through the window, making sure.

By that time, Bolan had already gained the patio and was approaching the glass sliding doors. The room beyond was dark, but he saw movement, hoping for an instant that it was his own reflection in the glass, deciding otherwise as bullets started punching through the tall doors, spraying jagged slivers as they came.

He hit the deck and leveled the Galil, sighting on muzzle-flashes as he started to fire back. The rifle had no automatic mode, but it was fast enough on semiauto for his needs. Two gunners fired at him, and he used six rounds to silence them, man-shadows lurching with the impact of his bullets, reeling, going down.

The way was open, but Bolan hesitated, glancing back in the direction he had come from. There was something, but...

There! A solitary figure was racing toward the long, detached garage. Bolan didn't recognize the profile, had no reason to believe the runner was one of the men he sought, but there was a shout behind the runner, and he recognized *that* voice.

Chris Stone was following the stranger, calling out, "Rahman, goddammit! Stop!" Instead of slowing, the runner poured on extra speed.

Bolan was turning back toward the garage, about to join the party, when a bullet slammed into his back, between the shoulder blades, and pitched him forward on his face.

BOULARD WAS PERFECTLY convinced that he would die at any moment, with the bullets swarming angrily around him. On the grass beside him lay a dead man, one of Malleville's thugs, blood welling darkly from an empty socket where his left eye should have been. Boulard supposed the hit had been a lucky accident, since no one would be capable of pinpoint fire in these conditions.

Would they?

Never one to take unnecessary chances, he refrained from standing, and started to crawl toward the mansion on his belly, feet and elbows digging at the lawn. Boulard had nearly panicked when the limousine had come charging at him, right across the mangled lawn, but it had swerved in search of other targets, mowing down two more of Malleville's people as he watched.

The major kept crawling. By the time the limo driver tired of running over people and decided he should shoot some, Boulard had reached the shrubs beside the house and was proceeding in a westerly direction, staying low, stopping and feigning death whenever he suspected he was being watched. In truth, with all the shooting going on, it was unlikely that he would be noticed. Those he passed by, sprawled out on the lawn, were either dead or badly wounded, and they showed no interest in his progress as he crept toward the patio.

Boulard had lost the borrowed Uzi after firing only half a dozen rounds and hitting no one. He was startled when a bullet struck the weapon from his hands, and had decided he was better off crawling past corpses than persisting in a stand-up fight with men who had him both outnumbered and outgunned. He had his pistol still, the standard-issue PA 15 MAB, with two spare magazines, a total of forty-six bullets in all. He clutched it tightly in one clammy fist and prayed he wouldn't have to use it out here, in the open, where his enemies were armed with submachine guns and automatic rifles.

Each time he slithered past a dead or wounded man, Boulard made sure to check the face. Each time he hoped that it would be Afif Rahman or the American, Stone. So far, he had seen no one that he recognized, and by the time he reached the corner of the house, Boulard could only wonder what had happened to his famous luck.

It was essential that Rahman and Stone should both be killed. If either one of them survived, there was a chance that he would talk—sometime, somewhere—about his dealings with Boulard and the Republic of Seychelles. The major's superiors had made it crystal clear that they would tolerate no more adverse publicity about their special visitors, particularly if it should include mass murder in the nation's capital. The deaths were one thing, but exposure of the killing to a worldwide audience was something to be avoided at all cost.

Or else.

Boulard hadn't inquired as to precisely what "or else" might mean. He understood the meaning well enough. If the disaster of this day went public, his superiors would need a scapegoat, someone they could sacrifice to make themselves look squeaky-clean. As the appointed chaperon to those in question, Boulard would have to fill that role. No arguments and no exemptions. If he couldn't solve the problem by himself, he would become part of the ultimate solution, with a show trial, manufactured evidence—in short, the works.

He could prevent all that, however, by eliminating his two charges, making sure that neither one could breathe a word to journalists—or breathe at all, for that matter. Boulard had never killed a man before, but he decided it would be a pleasure, just this once. Or maybe twice.

He was about to round the corner, hoping it was safe to stand up when he reached the patio, when gunfire suddenly exploded just in front of him, accompanied by sounds of smashing glass. It lasted only for a moment, but the sounds were close enough to send new tremors rippling through his body, making Boulard clutch his pistol in both hands to keep his grip. He couldn't crawl that way, however, and it was imperative that he find out exactly what was going on, discover if he had a way inside the house or if he had to look elsewhere.

Cautiously, reluctantly, he peeked around the corner, saw a tall man dressed in black, his face and hands painted black, staring through the shattered glass doors fronting on the patio. Instead of entering the house, however, the grim apparition turned, glanced back across the lawn and spotted something that attracted his attention. Boulard couldn't see what he was looking at—the man himself was in the way, blocking his view—nor did the major care. It mattered only that the hulking man had his back turned, that he was oblivious to danger on his flank.

It was an easy shot, one round between the shoulder blades, where it would clip his spine and leave him paralyzed, perhaps bore on to find the heart, or shatter into fragments, tearing through the lungs, cutting through major veins and arteries. To hell with Western movies, where the so-called good guys always faced their adversaries in the middle of an empty street, trusting to speed and courage for their victory.

Boulard would take the safe shot every time.

The major scrambled to his feet and stepped around the corner, out of sight from those still fighting on the lawn. He didn't recognize the man or understand why he was dressed in black, unless he was supposed to be a sentry in the woods around the house, drawn back by sounds of gunfire from the mansion. But in that case, whom had he been shooting at inside the house?

A glance through shattered doors revealed two bodies tangled on the carpet of a one-time game room, lying near a billiard table that was covered with a simple linen sheet. More strangers, but he knew they weren't Malleville's men, which meant they had to be two of the defenders. But in that case—

He was turning back to face the stranger he had killed, when suddenly the man rolled over, sat up and aimed a stubby submachine gun at him. The weapon's suppressor came close to doubling its length, and in the last split second of his life, Boulard was conscious of the fact that no one but his executioner would even hear him die.

He tried to raise his pistol, take the bastard with him if he couldn't save himself, but he was out of time. It felt as if a truck had rammed into his chest, pinning his body to the wall, and then he felt himself begin to slide.

So dark, the major told himself. So dark.

AFIF RAHMAN FUMBLED the keys and dropped them, ducking and catching them halfway to the floor. If there had been someone to see him, they would probably have complimented him on his agility, but he was all alone.

Not quite.

Stone was behind him somewhere, drawing closer by the heartbeat, and Rahman knew the American had bloody vengeance on his mind. Why else would he be here? Rahman wondered if Stone had organized this raid against his hideaway, but instantly dismissed the thought. Where would he find the men and the equipment? No, it had to be someone else—the hunters who had tracked him from America, perhaps—but Rahman didn't care.

The only thing he cared about right now was getting out.

Muhammad Alhazred was dead. Rahman had seen him cut down by a burst of automatic fire while he was trying to reorganize their handful of surviving troops. It should have felt strange, knowing he was dead, but there had been too many others, fellow *fedayeen* lost in the struggle, for another death to register in Rahman's mind.

Besides, the only life that really mattered to him was his own.

Stone fired a short burst through the open door of the three-car garage, but it was high, the bullets striking somewhere overhead. Rahman tried once more with the key and got it right this time. He slid in behind the sports car's steering wheel and jammed another key into the vehicle's ignition slot.

If he could only get past Stone, the rest would be what the Americans were pleased to call a piece of cake. The driveway he would follow placed the house between him and the soldiers fighting on the grass. Running without his lights, he should be at the gates and through them by the time his hasty exit was discovered. Most of them would never even know that he had fled until they started to search through the house, comb the grounds.

There would be questions later, an inquiry of some kind, but he would be long gone. Alhazred had hired the gunmen, and since he was dead—

Stone's second burst was closer, one round glancing off the sports car's roof with a hellacious clanging sound. Rahman switched on the engine, felt its power as he shifted into first, eased off the brake, his left foot riding on the clutch. More gas, and he was rolling, gaining speed. Suddenly Chris Stone stood there in front of him.

Rahman switched on his high beams, hoping the light

would blind Stone long enough to let him run down the mercenary, but Stone was ready for him. The American was firing two guns now, an Uzi in his right hand, and some kind of pistol in his left, both spitting fire.

Something pierced the windshield, struck him in the throat, and suddenly Rahman discovered that he couldn't breathe. A heartbeat later, as he lifted both hands from the steering wheel to clutch his throat, the whole windshield exploded in his face. He stood on the accelerator without meaning to, his body arching in the driver's seat until his pelvis jammed against the steering wheel. The sports car swerved and took off on a long, erratic charge across the lawn.

BOLAN WAS on his feet and moving when the sportster crashed into the tree line and the engine died. He rolled his shoulders, felt the bruise between them, where the Kevlar bulletproof vest had stopped the round that should have killed him. It hadn't absorbed all of the impact, though, and he would have a bruise to show for his near brush with death.

Chris Stone was standing in the middle of the broad south lawn, watching the sports car as it shuddered to a halt. He moved in that direction, following the double row of tire tracks in the grass, apparently intent on making sure the man behind the wheel was finished. That kind of determination indicated a relationship, and Bolan guessed that half his work was done.

He followed Stone, teeth clenched against the dizziness that came and went, left over from the impact that had slammed him to the deck a moment earlier. In Hollywood, the actors took imaginary hits to Kevlar vests and jumped up ready for a marathon, as if they hardly felt the slugs at all. In real life, it was more like living through a brutal beating, and the damage could include cracked bones, even internal injuries. As far as Bolan could tell without an X ray, he was all right, but he would feel the hit for days to come.

And right now, at this moment, he needed all the speed and the agility that he could muster.

Stone was standing by the sports car, peering through the window on the driver's side, when Bolan hailed him from a range of thirty yards. The mercenary straightened and turned to face him, standing with a gun in each hand, muzzles pointed toward the ground.

"Belasko."

"Close enough," Bolan said.

"Christ, you get around." If he was startled, Stone concealed it well. "I'd like to have your frequent-flier miles."

"You won't be needing them."

"That's where you're wrong," the mercenary said. "Now that I'm finished here, I figure that I owe myself a holiday."

"Too late for that. You should have gone for it before you joined the Paul Reveres."

"A job's a job," Stone said. "Somebody's paying you for this, I'll bet."

"I'm on my own."

"An altruist? I'm sure." The cynicism came through loud and clear. "Hell, maybe you're a saint."

"No," Bolan told him. "Just a soldier. Who's your friend?"

Stone glanced back at the car. "Oh, him? Your standard-issue terrorist. He decided it was easier to pay me with a bullet than the money we'd agreed on. I was forced to show him he was wrong."

"You live and learn," Bolan said.

"Not this time." Stone smiled. "So, what comes next?

Is this where I'm supposed to see the error of my ways and make a full confession? Maybe let you put the handcuffs on?"

"No handcuffs," Bolan said.

"I didn't think so." Still, he hesitated. "Are you sure you want to do this? We could still forget about it, go our separate ways."

"Can't do it," Bolan told him.

"Well, in that case—"

Stone was slick, no doubt about it, but the move was in his eyes before he made it. Bolan saw it there and raised his MP-5 K, holding down the trigger from the time its muzzle reached a level with Stone's knees. The parabellum shockers stitched a ragged line of holes across his torso, from the groin up to the neck, the last rounds ripping through his throat and lower jaw. He tumbled over backward, firing both guns as he fell, the bullets wasted on a velvet tropic sky.

A distant wail of sirens reached the Executioner's ears, becoming louder by the moment. He glanced back toward the house, where sounds of battle sputtered on, survivors of the first clash fighting to the bitter end. He left them to it, hoping that the riot squad could mop it up without incurring any casualties.

The long hunt over, Bolan turned and jogged back toward the tree line and his waiting rental car. He still had far to go, but he was on his way.

And to the Executioner, that said it all.

EPILOGUE

"Some kind of wild-ass scheme they had," Brognola said, "to pull off raids across the South, all at the same time, if they could. They had a list of targets, more or less what you'd expect. Some churches, synagogues, a couple of newspapers, legal offices, some individuals."

"What happened?" Bolan asked him, facing the big Fed across the table of a fast-food restaurant in Savannah, Georgia, with a mug of steaming coffee in his hand.

"The Bureau started making some arrests the day you left for the Seychelles," Hal said. "They bagged some Paul Reveres, some yahoos from the ASA, whatever. It's a given with these redneck types. Somebody always tries to cut a deal."

"They talked," Bolan said.

"Loud and clear. Enough of them to wrap it up, at least. We didn't get them all in time, of course. The way they had it set, no one man knew all of the targets or the other guys involved. Enough of them were still at large to burn a church in Vicksburg, Mississippi, and a lawyer's office in Montgomery. He's been suing Kluxers every time they whip somebody's ass. Already put two Klans into receivership. He won't be out of action long, from what I hear. The rest of them—I make it thirty-five or forty guys, all told—are looking at a list of state and federal charges that'll have them in and out of court for years."

"The guy Stone wasted at the villa?"

"Interpol advises me that he was one Afif Rahman, some kind of field agent for Hezbollah. The way it reads, they wanted some way to attack America without their own hands getting dirty—or at least without the media suspecting who had called the shots. It was your basic whammy—nice domestic terrorism, with a right-wing angle that would add insult to injury."

"Rahman was running it alone?"

"Stateside, we're pretty sure. If he had anybody helping him, we don't know who they were. It works best as a two-man deal, Rahman and Stone. Pike never knew what hit him, thinking Stone was so true-blue. He had the bastard lined up as his heir apparent if he ever left the Paul Reveres."

"And how's the colonel doing?" Bolan asked.

"He didn't make it," Brognola replied without elaboration.

"Tough."

"I'm crying on the inside."

Bolan had reserved the final question, not wanting to rush it, making sure his tone was casual. "And what about the lady?"

"Ginger Ross?" Brognola shrugged and glanced out the window toward the sunbaked parking lot. "She's on the mend. I couldn't tell you what her future is with ATF. She broke a lot of rules, and last I heard, she wasn't any too contrite."

"She had her reasons," Bolan stated.

"It may not be enough. I'll see what I can do, but I don't have a lot of pull in that department."

"Anything would help."

"No promises," Brognola cautioned. "You know…ah, hell, forget it."

"What?"

"It's nothing."

"Would you spit it out already?" Bolan prompted.

"Well, I understand she's got some downtime, while they're setting up the formal hearing. Not exactly R&R, but still…"

"I don't think so."

"Me, neither. Hell, you'd have to look her name up in the D.C. phone book, go to all that trouble. What's the point?"

"She's got enough heat as it is."

"No doubt."

They sat in silence for a moment, sipping coffee, Bolan watching as a tanker truck rolled by outside.

"D.C., you said."

"It's warming up," Brognola said. "We're looking forward to an early spring."

Bolan was staring through his own reflection in the window, looking past the ghostlike image, when he cracked a smile.

**Don't miss out on the action in these titles featuring
THE EXECUTIONER®, STONY MAN™ and SUPERBOLAN®!**

The Red Dragon Trilogy

#64210	FIRE LASH	$3.75 U.S.	☐
		$4.25 CAN.	☐
#64211	STEEL CLAWS	$3.75 U.S.	☐
		$4.25 CAN.	☐
#64212	RIDE THE BEAST	$3.75 U.S.	☐
		$4.25 CAN.	☐

Stony Man™

#61910	FLASHBACK	$5.50 U.S.	☐
		$6.50 CAN.	☐
#61911	ASIAN STORM	$5.50 U.S.	☐
		$6.50 CAN.	☐
#61912	BLOOD STAR	$5.50 U.S.	☐
		$6.50 CAN.	☐

SuperBolan®

#61452	DAY OF THE VULTURE	$5.50 U.S.	☐
		$6.50 CAN.	☐
#61453	FLAMES OF WRATH	$5.50 U.S.	☐
		$6.50 CAN.	☐
#61454	HIGH AGGRESSION	$5.50 U.S.	☐
		$6.50 CAN.	☐

(limited quantities available on certain titles)

TOTAL AMOUNT	$
POSTAGE & HANDLING	$
($1.00 for one book, 50¢ for each additional)	
APPLICABLE TAXES*	$ _____
TOTAL PAYABLE	$ _____
(check or money order—please do not send cash)	

To order, complete this form and send it, along with a check or money order for the total above, payable to Gold Eagle Books, to: **In the U.S.:** 3010 Walden Avenue, P.O. Box 9077, Buffalo, NY 14269-9077; **In Canada:** P.O. Box 636, Fort Erie, Ontario, L2A 5X3.

Name:_____

Address:_____ City:_____

State/Prov.:_____ Zip/Postal Code: _____

*New York residents remit applicable sales taxes.
 Canadian residents remit applicable GST and provincial taxes.

GOLD
EAGLE®

GEBACK18

James Axler

OUTLANDERS™

Trained by the ruling elite of post-holocaust America as a pureheart warrior, Kane is an enemy of the order he once served. He knows of his father's fate, he's seen firsthand the penalties, and yet a deep-rooted instinct drives him on to search for the truth. An exile to the hellzones, an outcast, Kane is the focus of a deadly hunt. But with brother-in-arms Grant, and Brigid Baptiste, keeper of the archives, he's sworn to light the dark past...and the world's fate. New clues hint that a terrifying piece of the puzzle is buried in the heart of Asia, where a descendant of the Great Khan wields awesome powers....

Available September 1997,
wherever Gold Eagle books are sold.